About the Author

Kathleen Coyle was born in Derry in 1886. While working for
The Statesman in London in the early years of the twentieth
century, she was exposed to the burgeoning socialist movement and the campaign for women's suffrage. A short marriage
in Dublin was not a success, and she returned to London with
her two children in 1920. Her first two novels, *Piccadilly* and
The Widow's House, were published in 1923 and 1924 repec-
tively, and succeeded in earning her the funds that enabled her
to move to the continent with her children. From 1926 to 1936,
she lived in France, moving on the fringes of celebrity and
publishing nine novels, several short stories and a psycho-
logical fantasy. Of this period her most lauded works are *Liv*
and *A Flock of Birds* (reissued by Wolfhound Press, 1995). *A
Flock of Birds* was a runner-up to E.M. Forster's *A Passage to
India* for a major literary award and was translated into both
French and Italian. Some of her short stories also appeared in
French literary magazines. In 1937, she moved to the United
States, settling in Greenwich Village, New York. During the
Second World War, she placed many of her stories with the
Redbook Magazine. Kathleen moved to Princeton, New Jersey,
in the late 1940s, where she worked consistently although her
health was failing. She died on 25 March 1952 with a number of
projects unfinished. Her body of publications by then included
thirteen full-length novels, a novella, some anecdotal tales,
several short stories and a volume of autobiography, *The
Magical Realm* (reissued by Wolfhound Press, 1997).

To the memory of
Ingertha Sviggum of Arendal

Liv

Kathleen Coyle

WOLFHOUND PRESS

This edition published in 2000 by
Wolfhound Press Ltd
68 Mountjoy Square
Dublin 1, Ireland
Tel: (353-1) 874 0354
Fax: (353-1) 872 0207

First edition Jonathan Cape, 1928

This book is fiction. All characters, incidents and names have no connection
with any persons living or dead. Any apparent resemblance is purely
coincidental.

 Wolfhound Press receives financial assistance from the Arts
Council/An Chomhairle Ealaíon, Dublin.

British Library Cataloguing in Publication Data
A catalogue record for this book is available from the British Library.

ISBN 0-86327-811-6

10 9 8 7 6 5 4 3 2 1

Cover Illustration: 'The Window' by Letitia Marion Hamilton ARHA (1878–1964),
    courtesy of Pyms Gallery, London. Copyright Major Charles Hamilton
Cover Design: Mark O'Neill
Typeset in Belwe Light by Wolfhound Press
Printed in the Republic of Ireland by ColourBooks, Dublin.

Chapter One

When the body of old Pastor Evensen was carried out of the house to its last resting-place, his widow, Anna, watched it in silence, with wide eyes and with senses completely sundered from any vision of the old, old man who had been her husband. She was thinking that, at last, she would be able to go on the visit to Sonja. Sonja was her sister. She had not seen her for twenty years. Five years after she had married the Pastor Evensen, she had gone with her two little girls — Liv, aged four, and Astrid, aged two — to visit Sonja in her distant home in the Sulitelma mountains. She frowned as she stood there, thinking of it, thinking of Liv. She was puzzled about Liv, by the girl's desire to make the grand tour. So many of the young Norwegians did that. Sonja had done it. It rose like a sort of protection in her mind that it was possible that Sonja would be able to prevent Liv.

Liv and Astrid had quite forgotten the former visit, but they were aware, in a manner so subtle that it could only be illustrated by upraised hands in their mother's drawing-room and a certain tone in the voices — 'Sonja! Isn't it incredible?' — that there existed some inexplicable motive for Aunt Sonja's devotion (she never absented herself) to her household, her husband and her five sons. All they knew was that she had married a man who owned mines in the Sulitelma district, and that she lived in the Rindalsholm in the mountains, and was apparently happy.

It was not until the end of July that they were able to go. On the eve of their departure, Harald Christensen rode over from the Mornesund farm. He tied his horse to the well-post in the courtyard and came up to the day-house and shouted, without going in: 'Lee ... af! Lee ... af!'

Liv opened the drawing-room door and stood, smiling down the stretch of hall to him: 'Goodness!' she answered in her soft contralto voice, 'here I am!' Her tall figure was stooped towards him, her head, drooping forward a little, gave her the poise of a flower.

He looked black on the threshold, with the sunlight behind him, one-dimensional, as though he were cut out in black paper. His hair was ruffled, standing up in a bush. He came towards her, losing the blackness as he approached and coming out, very blond and solid in the shady hall. His blue eyes, fixed on her, were troubled, full of hunger and heaviness. 'Liv,' he said, 'come out with me into the field, come? I have something to say to you!'

Her smile melted, vanished. 'No,' she said, almost sullenly, but the sweetness of her expression remained untouched by her refusal, 'I can't. Can't you say it to me here?'

She went back into the drawing-room, and he followed her to the window that looked out on the town. The deep blue waters lay in the fjord as in a basin.

'Oh, Harald!' she cried, 'don't ask me again!'

'I must.' Behind her he saw the portrait of a very ancient Pastor Evensen with his three wives in a row beside him. The smile on the old priest's face, smirking amidst his spouses, maddened him. The blood rushed up under his blond skin, turning his face rosy under its tan and making his hair absurdly fair. 'Look here, Liv, will you…?'

She finished it for him, '…marry you?' She moved away from him, and stood quiet against the bright curtains. After a moment she spoke: 'You know that I don't want to marry … not yet … I want to travel.…'

'Your father was always against that idea.' The tone in which he said it defied her to forget her father's refusal.

'No,' she met his challenge, 'he did not understand. I must go. I must. I want to know what … what it means.'

'What what means?' He tried to tie her down, confound her with a limitation.

She swept the limitation away: 'Life!' The vexed, troubled look in his blue eyes made her consider him, 'everybody isn't content like you, Harald.…'

'I'm not content!'

'Oh, I know!' There were such variations in desire. She added dogmatically: 'I can't pretend.'

'I don't want you to pretend. You know you love me.'

'Yes … I love Astrid, too.' She placed the matter upon a plane beyond distinctions. She was shocked, startled out of her air of indifference by the sudden passionate sweep of his voice.

'Liv, will you, or will you not marry me?' He took hold of her and made her turn so that she was compelled to meet his look.

She felt sorry for him, and was tender, wanting to assuage him: 'I do care, but not like that.… I want you to be happy.'

'You will marry me?'

She looked steadily into his eyes, conscious that her beauty wounded him. She could not help it. She did not want to be used like that, to rouse or cheat him. Very slowly she said, just as though he was a small boy asking her to make up a game with him, 'Perhaps, but not now, Harald, not for...' and in her mind she finished it — years and years. By then, perhaps, he would no longer need her. He might find somebody else.

'I take that as a promise.' He still held her, strongly, so that she should not feel the tremor in his arms.

'A half promise.'

'A promise,' he repeated.

'Then you must wait!'

'I'll wait.'

'Years and years and years.'

'I'll wait until I get you,' he said stubbornly.

His stubbornness broke her pity as though it were courage. She was released by it, free with him. The rigidity went out of her. She put her hands spontaneously on his shoulders and kissed him, as she had kissed him often, on his cheek. 'There!' she said, a rasp of tenderness in her deep voice, 'I'm not worth waiting for!'

He did not kiss her. His grip slackened and he let her go. They stood together gazing through the window at the sunlight lying upon the town of Odda, at the queer bending trees, and the tranquil, profound fjord. A servant came out and clattered across the yard, pausing to caress Harald's horse, then disappeared into a doorway.

Fru Evensen said behind him: 'Why, you're here, Liv! I thought that you had gone out to buy those travelling straps!'

'No, Astrid went.'

Harald was bowing clumsily before Fru Evensen. 'Liv is going to marry me.'

She did not seem to believe it. She looked from him to Liv, perplexed.

'Not really, Mother. I've said it to keep him quiet.'

He repeated it. 'She is going to marry me.'

The boy was flushed and determined. There was a new will in him which changed him in that moment before Anna Evensen's eyes into a young man who was a stranger to her. She seemed to lose him. He escaped from her. 'Well, well!' she exclaimed, accepting the situation as it was, 'I shouldn't wonder. When you were both babies, and I used to go over to Mornesund, your mother and I said often that perhaps one day you would marry. You were so stupid, Harald, as a baby, so fat, and you wouldn't stop crawling. Liv was on her feet long before you, she was so agile, she was able ... you may not believe it, to turn her legs right round from back to front, make a wheel on the floor ... she was double-jointed.'

She was talking foolishly, stupidly, the boy thought, but he took a quick comfort from the knowledge that his dead mother had wanted him to marry Liv, even at the stage when she was making wheels of her legs on the floor. He felt oddly rough and strong between the two women in their black dresses, secure. It made him say to Liv, aware that he was in danger of overdoing the assurance, 'you see, it has been meant from the beginning.'

She felt angry with him, truly angry with him, and with her mother. They seemed to want to force her into his possession. It drove her into saying: 'It is a good thing that we are going to visit Aunt Sonja.'

Fru Evensen sat down upon the yellow sofa. Her blackness made a great dark pool in the yellow brightness, and there came into Liv's mind a ridiculous remembrance, ridiculous because it had nothing at all to do with any of them, of the parting of the waters in the Red Sea and the tribal hosts going through to victory. She laughed. And instantly she was aware that Harald thought that she was laughing at him. 'Something absurd,' she explained, 'came into my mind.' He remained uncertain how to take her. 'Why, why, oh why don't you want to marry Astrid? She'd be much better at Mornesund than me,' she cried to him.

'Astrid is not you.' He put continents of praise into the words.

'That's true,' Fru Evensen nodded. 'Astrid's plain. She takes after me. You, Liv ... you resemble Sonja, Sonja at your age.'

Liv stared at her mother. It was the first time that she had ever been compared to Aunt Sonja. Remotely, without cohesion, she connected the comparison with her father. She saw her father, far away in everlasting space, nodding to her and smiling just as her mother was nodding and smiling. Her mother, sitting in her black dress on the yellow sofa, and Harald Christensen, who wanted to marry her, ceased to be there. There was nobody present but her father nodding his assent to the fact that she resembled her Aunt Sonja.

Astrid came, glowing from out-of-doors into the room. 'Oh!' she exclaimed when she saw them all together, and greeted Harald. She undid the straps and showed them to her mother: 'I met Barbra Grondahl in Vorings, and, what do you think, she's going back again to Paris, after all. She asked me to tell you.'

'I knew already,' Liv answered, and answered savagely, 'some people have all the luck.'

'I don't see any *luck* in it,' Fru Evensen corrected as she watched Astrid curl the straps into a spring that shot out every time she reached the buckle.

Liv was silent. She had again turned to the window, which was open, and the bruised odour of the flowers came up to her. Two girls in red Hardanger bodices were walking in the distance across Henrik Mitten's cornfield. The corn was reaped and stooked, and the girls threaded their way through the stooks like two poppies. Tomorrow they were going. There was a line in her aunt's letter — the blue-berries will be ripe on Stortoppen. The blue-berries would be ripe in the high, dark frosty mountains. Harald and her mother were telling Astrid that she was going to marry him. Astrid's laughter, heard behind, was very sweet, with a catch in it like a stream running over stones. Astrid was very fond of Harald. It was all wrong that he should not marry her.

'You must give her a ring.'

Liv took it in like ice. The garden, the summer, the blood in her body cooled into apprehension. Before it came she knew what was coming. He was going to give her a ring, make a rite of it, and for some reason that defeated her and was incomprehensible she was conscious that she would not be able to refuse. He was beside her and he was saying: 'I brought it.... It belonged to my mother.' She knew then that it was Fru Christensen's silver ring set with sapphires. She had loved that ring on Fru Christensen's finger, and now he was going to give it to her. It was a fairy ring. It had always made an image for her of a silver gateway in a fairy story, filled with the purple of the twilight. She had sat at Fru Christensen's knee listening to fairy stories ... all the human elements passing through silver gateways into the purpled highways of adventure. Harald was giving her the ring. She wished that Fru Christensen was alive and not dead and stretched in Odda Graveyard. She rose in secret mutiny against Harald, who wanted this marriage-love from her. But what was the use of wishing? She pushed her hand through her hair and smoothed it, then spread her fingers over her ear as though she could shut out what he was going to say to her. He said nothing. He took down her hand and put the ring on her finger. There was a great silence in the room at her back, and it seemed to her that Fru Christensen was there with the others. She turned to meet them, lifting her spirit against them like a shield, and was humbled, contrite, as though all her sins were exposed to them. She said: 'I ought not to take it.'

'You might,' said her mother, 'thank him more prettily than that.'

Astrid was taking off her hat before the mirror. She pretended not to hear what Fru Evensen had said to Liv. She chuckled: 'Oh!' she cried, as if she did not know that Harald had given his mother's ring to Liv and got no thanks for it, 'Barbra *is* funny. She told me such a story, perhaps you've already heard it, Liv. When she was fifteen, and at the high school in Oslo, one day she went into a public telephone-box and called up Per Andersen, the town engineer ... you know how ugly he is, his face all over spots, and she began like this, in a strange voice, simpering, so that he might take her for some servant girl: "Is that you?" "Yes, yes," he said, quite simply. "Oh do, *do* forgive me for calling you up like this, but I had to, I positively had to speak to you. Will you forgive me? Do say that you forgive me." He answered "Yes, yes; it's nothing," but he sounded quite cross. "Don't be cross," she begged, "but I've seen you so often, I felt I should die if I could not speak to you. Do you know, I have a special name for you!" Of course he was flattered. She could feel him being flattered at the other end. You know how conceited he is, all pomp and circumstance, as Barbra says. Well he said: "No, no! I'm not cross. Tell me, tell me what is the special name?" "You're sure you won't be angry?" ... She was quite exasperating. "No, no! Of course not." "Well then," she told him, simpering and pretending to be most fearfully embarrassed: "I call you ... sheep!"'

'Oh, Astrid!' Liv exclaimed, 'No! She never told me that.'

Even Fru Evensen laughed, although she said immediately: 'What a naughty girl. What a bold girl!' and she went back to Harald. The boy troubled her. He was not a boy now, he was a strange young man, and his smile was a mask. She beckoned to him to sit beside her, and she put her white, gentle hand on his knee. 'It will be all right, Harald; do not fret, my boy. When you were two little toddling creatures, we planned, your mother and I, that it would be just so, just so. It will come all right. Be patient. Liv is a foolish girl.' She smiled across him at Liv.

Liv knew that the smile was meant for him and not for her. She was in a rage against her mother for scolding her before Harald, scolding her to him, as though she had been naughty, like Barbra Grondahl in the telephone-box. She felt angry, boiling with anger, and she hated the ring on her finger. She longed to take it off and throw it from her. She didn't want it. But quick as her anger raced, it ebbed, and

she seemed to be very close to Fru Christensen, years ago
— it was so difficult to think of people as dead — in
Mornesund, very close and standing with her in sunshine in a
field that had tiny pearl-like flowers in it, with the wind
blowing. It was mysterious. It restrained her. She came back
again to the bright drawing-room and the figure of Astrid,
trailing the parcel-string across the floor for the kitten, and
Harald sitting by the black pool of her mother's dress on the
yellow sofa, being petted because he wanted to marry her. She
was startled by her own voice making the oddest avowal: 'I am
only trying to be honest, Mother. If I can, I will. There, Harald,
you'll have to be content with that!' She was neither content
nor certain within herself. Something deep down in her
seemed to have risen to bear witness against her own desires,
arisen to appease Fru Christensen's ghost and give hope to her
son. The act of living enlarged itself in her consciousness,
making mountains out of molehills, and somersaulting upon
her the importance of her dreams. The actual became near
and terrible, even the tiny kitten, crouched and ready to
spring on the carpet, became exaggerated, dangerous. And
none of them really meant anything. They were significant
for nothing. She shivered and moved over amongst them,
saying, in a hushed voice, 'Oh, Astrid! I wish I were you.'

'So do I,' said the happy girl, and went on playing with the
kitten.

Liv's mood endured. Going away next day in the little
steamer that carried them through the Sorfjorden, the little
town of her birth and upbringing (with Harald lost in the
bunch of human flies in the foreground), seemed extremely
big and clear, as though it stood out before rain, clear before

the mists came that were to hide it; it grew bigger, as it faded, with memories. The red and white houses raised their roofed heads to her with the strong July sunset shining in their windows like tears. Dark patches of tilled lands ran through the landscape. On the cliffs, on the Trollheim road above her home, the tall conifers stood in hosts. She wondered then if it was love that she felt for this place from which she had prayed to God to escape. And again she was frightened, and cheated of understanding. It took the glory out of liberty, made it also a defenceless city from which she might have to cry out for unrealised protections. They passed a valley lit with the morning, the fertile Hardanger morning. Earth drank the sunlight. A pack of goats, minute and distant, tended by a minute goat-herd, skipped in the verdant valley, and reminded her of the El Greco print in her father's study. There was the same force of diminished beings dripping with life before a vast background. It made mankind out to be no better, when seen far enough off, than a troop of sparrows. How did her father take that text? Making poetry to heaven! Something about no sparrow that could falter or fail without God's knowledge. Tiny little sparrows fluttering in the bowls of the valleys of the world…. Harald had been pleased because she had caressed his horse. He had laid his cheek against the brute's nozzle where her own had been. Harald made her appear hard. She had to be hard, to hold herself against his sentiment. But within she was not hard — only frightened.

Her mother touched her sleeve. 'Liv, what are you thinking about?'

She hesitated, and remarked: 'I was thinking about father, what lovely sermons he used to preach.'

'That is true.' Long, long ago Anna Evensen had been jealous of those sermons. They had excluded her from her husband's mind, made a chapel of his thoughts wherein she was never able to enter. He was a great Christian. It made him somewhat inhuman, failing towards her as a man. He was so very, very clever, so spiritual, a dreamer, he forgot the things that make up the sum of life, the sum of daily life. He was a daily lost lamb to her. She was always rescuing him, making it possible for his wonderful but wandering brain to fulfil itself. He forgot her, and she had to be content to be forgotten, but she was there all the time, rescuing him. She was finer than he because she had more sympathy. Without her, she knew, he would have strayed so far that nobody would have understood him. It was she who said always: remember that they are little children ... unless ye become as little children ... and he had remembered to give them the beauty simply, sowing it like a periwinkle in the rocky fastnesses of their hearts. And, for all that, it was she who had paid. 'Yes, Liv, he was a great preacher, he was full of dreams, he had the prophet's touch.'

'It is only now that I begin to understand him. Before, I ... I never noticed.'

'That is quite natural, my child. There is nothing to regret. He was an old man when you were born. He was too old for you to have known him.'

Nevertheless the regret was there, in Liv's thoughts. She was too young for the judgment. She had given him so little. 'I might have given him more.'

'There is still time,' Anna Evensen assured her, 'and you must not forget that your beauty was a constant joy to him.'

He had had his fill of the girl's youth. Liv was his darling. She had his own moods, although too young to recognise them. He had wasted no crumb of the recognition.

'Do you know, Mother, I feel as if everything, everything — us and Harald, even places, even what I believe in — is changing. Is it because he has died?'

'Nonsense!' said Fru Evensen sharply, 'that is stupid.' She fought against the sense of change because she also was acutely aware of it. She did not want to admit it. It was as if barricades had gone down and she, a prisoner, was once more out of the cage, in flight. She was going to see Sonja. She was able to go. She could stay as long as she wished, and she need not return until she truly desired to return. The freedom was still raw. She was not enjoying it. It was still a fair prospect, more than a relief, and like Liv, secretly it unsteadied her. The unsteadiness drew them together, made them kindred and glowing as they stood there together. In a moment the tie passed and they were separate again. Liv was watching the snow of gulls on the crags and her thoughts were hidden. She sought for Astrid as for solace and was comforted by the girl's responsive laughter, by the quick thrust of her arm through hers: 'Oh, Mother, I am enjoying this! It's a great adventure!'

It was an adventure for all three of them, the end of a past of long duration which could never, now that it was broken, ever be repieced. It was done with. The future, like the voyage, was before them. They were certain of Sonja's welcome. Beyond that they could not be quite certain. Standing between her two daughters, it seemed to her that the world could not really do anything very terrible to her. It had taught her birth and death. It had done its worst. She looked at Astrid's happy face and from her to Liv. Liv's eyes were still distant watching the flight of gulls on Eidekollen.

The excitement did not abate in Liv. She remained possessed by an exaggeration that lifted everything she came in contact with and multiplied it against her ears and eyes. Passing by the seven bridal sisters she was moved by such passionateness that the soul seemed to go out of her to embrace with full lips this place veiled in clouds that seemed to have rolled freshly from the feet of God. Heaven was so close upon the earth, the angels barely hidden. What was winter but the close fold of wings? What was the wind but a voice crying to the valleys to give up and to every living thing to submit? The heroes were there now, as they had ever been. Thought was primal. It made Fear so great that it became courage and the cloak of dignity. Kings were born daily in the mesh of those solitudes. Liv was rapt, humble before it. It affected her physically, filling her limbs with strange languor. The languor pulled through her clothes, making even the touch of her fine linen chemise against her skin feel like a caress. It was as though she walked naked through tall grasses on the high mountains feeling the meaning of the sun and the wind and the clouds rolling straight from God.

In contrast with the wonder that was going on within her, she was irritated by Astrid's childish chatter and her mother's over-anxiousness about food and the common-places of their fellow-passengers — the man with a moustache like a sweeping brush, and the pretty girl who spent one entire morning plucking her eyebrows, and flirting with an Irishman who told her that they'd put a curse on her in Connaught for plucking the living.

Chapter Two

n Rindalsholm, in her house perched above the valley, Sonja Krag awaited them. Her husband was absent. He had been obliged to go to Trondjem with Erik. Tore and Bernt and Georges were *en pension* in Trondjem, so that only she and Olaf would be there to greet them. The supper was prepared and yet they did not come. It grew late. She insisted upon Olaf taking his supper and not waiting for them, but she allowed him to stay up a little longer. She sat by the window with the boy at her knees telling him the old story of Birkbeins and the king's son. She told it in her own way, adding Franciscan touches of birds and beasts who were friendly to them as they passed, and of the strange sign of an arrow on a hemlock trunk, a golden arrow made by the sun on purpose to guide them. It was so still in the house. There was no sound except the sound of her voice telling the little boy about the deliverance of Haakon.

'And it wasn't a real arrow, an arrow...' he made the gesture with his hands, '...that you could break?'

'No, it was not real ... only a sign. It was marked quite clearly and in gold.' He never expected it to be real. It was he who had led her with his own inventions and encouragement to play this lovely game of imagination. None of the others — except Tore — had ever been like that. And Tore had come so close to the others in age that the trick had been spitted in him as it had sprung. With Olaf it was different; she had Olaf all to herself. She drew him to her and put her lips against his hair. It was peaceful when they were alone like this. Georges and Bernt were such noisy boys, Johan's boys. Tore belonged to each of them in turn. One side of him like Johan and the other completely hers. Olaf was still hers. He had not changed. She hoped that he would never change, always stay the dreamer that he was. It would preserve him, and keep him by her. But she loved them all. There was so much love in that house for her bestowal that at times she felt drained with it, heavy with life. She was grateful for these spells of idleness now with Olaf. Long ago she had dreaded illness. It struck ten. They counted the strokes. She thought: he must really go to bed. His eyes had that drowsy look in them which always came when she told him a story. And just as she was going to say to him that he must truly go to bed and not stay up a moment longer, they heard the far-off burr of a motor on the valley road.

'There!' he pressed excitedly against her, 'they're coming!'

The sun still burned on the edge of the world. The scatter of its setting was spread over the valley, its brows still showed. The air was lit from its reflection as from a hearth, a hearth which burned in summer. Far upon Stortoppen behind them was a crest of snow, and ice in the mountain runnels. She waited, draining up the dregs of her idleness, and then she sent Olaf down to the kitchen to tell Ingeborg that they were coming. She wondered if Anna would have changed much, what her girls were like. Of herself she thought not at all. Closed up into a burning red ring of the sunset, she saw the beauty of her son Olaf as he had gone out of the room. She waited for his return, and together they went out, and from the steps watched the black beetle-like car come slowly towards them until it reached their gate, and then make a quick dive to their steps. It was one of Olsen's cars, she saw, and remembered that that particular chauffeur made a habit of racing his car in short spaces. He treated it like a highly-mettled horse which he could rouse and curb at his will. Anna got out of the car backwards, because the step was high. To Sonja it was a stranger's back. Her behind, she thought sadly, is so big, and her shoulders had broadened and were so fleshy that they stooped. This was Anna whom she had known young. She was the same Anna when she turned, scarcely changed at all, agreeable and pleasant. The agreeableness and pleasantness seemed to have grown and become enlarged upon her. The slight, Japanese-faced dark girl beside her was just like her — like what she had been — and somehow more familiar. In the golden twilight air their black clothes looked tensely black as though they had gathered some dark substance and atmosphere into their folds.

'This is Astrid,' said Anna, taking the girl's hand and bringing her forward. 'Oh, my dear Sonja, your hair, your hair — it is quite white!' Anna's voice quavered. She was ready to cry.

Sonja smiled. She was drawn into her sister's arms and embraced. And then, turning to the girl Astrid, she also enfolded and embraced her. Her attention was drawn to Olaf, who was pulling his aunt up the steps, almost making her trip. 'Be careful, Olaf,' she cried to him, and took her sister's arm to aid her. Anna arrived panting, more from emotion than anything else, on the top step. Astrid was already friends with the boy. She was holding out a rug to him and saying:

'What shall I do with this ... put it on top of you?'

'Put it on top of me,' he answered, and she did. His laughter came out from underneath the rug and mingled with hers.

Sonja turned on the threshold, aware that she had forgotten something, and met Liv's eyes. The girl was standing, tall and still, on the gravel, watching her. 'You are Liv!' she said in her clear, peculiarly lucid tones, and held out her arms.

Liv hesitated for a second, then, holding her body erect as though she were partaking in a ceremony, she mounted the steps. Half-way up she paused, and she, too, held out her arms. They reached to each other without touching and neither of them moved. The movement was within them, drawing their eyes through each other's to read what they could find. Sonja was conscious of a bird stirring in the wood work somewhere above her, conscious of the peaked trees, cinder-black in the distance, there was a fume of vapour rising out of the motor bonnet — she was even able to reason in the flight of a second at the resemblance of brute and mechanical behaviour — and beyond, the long shore of fire in the sky over the trees, the broken arc of the sun. And at the same time she saw nothing but Liv's face transfigured and beautiful on the steps below her.

'Aunt Sonja!'

'My child!' she said gently, and took her into her arms.

It seemed to Liv that there came out of that brief contact in her aunt's arms some enveloping understanding that took in sky and earth, mountain and fjord, and every fragment of her own doubting, and gave them shelter. When she stood alone again she made a movement with her half-closed hand from her breast to arm's length, that was like the gesture of one taking place in a procession. The march was, in strange fashion, made for her. The lasting twilight burned behind her, reflecting her form in the glass of the inner doors as she passed through them.

Aunt Sonja showed them their rooms. She and Astrid were to share a room from which you could, Aunt Sonja made them listen, hear the roar of the foss in the distance. Farther along, with the windows facing in the opposite direction, was the guest-room which had been given to their mother.

Sonja waited while her sister took off her travelling cloak and hat. Anna was chattering like a magpie, a very matronly magpie, giving her absurd details about the journey and of the loss of her purse at Skjonsta. They had found it, after much searching, in the air-cushion cover. Astrid had buttoned it in by mistake ... she did everything so quickly, that girl. Sonja saw Liv standing in the doorway and smiled at her. She wanted to ask if she knew where her room was, and felt that it would be like telling her to go away, and said nothing. Liv was not dismissed by the smile, but she answered it and went away all the same. She looked at Anna, who was raking a comb through her front hair. 'What do you do, Anna,' she asked, 'with Liv?'

'My dear, I do nothing,' she replied volubly, 'just nothing. She is quite difficult ... mooning all the way up here, and as snappy as ginger if you asked her anything.'

'Doesn't she do anything ... herself?'

'She doesn't, I must tell the truth, know what she wants. She won't let herself want anything except to make...' she emphasised it with the silver gleam of the comb,' to make the grand tour!'

There was a tiny sparked silence, and then Sonja asked: 'For some reason ... to study perhaps?'

'Not she! Just, I assure you, to see the world!'

Sonja crossed over to the window and began to regulate the gathers in the netted blind. She said nothing. She heard Anna rubbing her nails. Then came what she expected.

'I was hoping that you would be able to ... to discourage, to put her off the idea.'

Again Sonja said nothing. The room, scarcely used and so much fresher than any other room in the house, was like a chapel of the virgin, with its blue and white paint. She wished the girls could have had it, but she gave it to Anna, as it was in front of the house and out of sound of the waterfall. The girls had blue eyes, quite different blues. Astrid's hair was dark like her mother's. Her eyes were not so wide open as Liv's, and they seemed lighter. That was in contrast to her hair. Liv's looked dark in her fair hair. She knew that she was thinking of these things as a blind against Anna's meaning. She wished she had not heard. But of course she had heard. It was quite clear what Anna wanted her to do. Stupid Anna.

'I don't mean,' said Anna, feeling that she had blundered and blundering more, 'that you should tell her anything special' (Sonja had never told any of them anything) 'but couldn't you dissuade her? It's only a notion she has got. After all, you can't believe that it is right for her to go ... if ... if she were your own daughter, now...' she got no farther. Sonja was looking at her so fixedly that it made her feel uncomfortable.

Sonja pitied her. 'How can I tell? ...' she answered the questions with one of her own. 'I do not know anything about her, absolutely nothing. It might be the best thing on earth for her to go....'

'It might!' Anna was sarcastic. 'Oh, Sonja, how can you?'

Sonja smoothed her. 'But come,' she said, with that slow gentleness that emanated from her like grace, 'you must be famished. We mustn't talk about such matters ... yet. There is plenty of time.' She was storing up trouble by the encouragement, she knew, but also she was gaining time to find out what to do about it. She gave Anna no time to begin again, for she added: 'I'll just peep into the girls' room to see if they're ready.'

Astrid was standing before the mirror, brandishing a comb, just as Anna had brandished hers. Liv was sitting on the bed with Olaf, her arm behind the boy, and a lost, inattentive expression on her face. The boy was whistling under his breath. His eyes were half-closed, his lips pursed. The window had been opened as though they wished to hear the Trangfoss singing its song to the night. The boy was the first to become conscious of Sonja's presence. He was indignant, roused immediately:

'Astrid doesn't believe in the golden arrow!' he shouted.

'Doesn't she?' she responded to him, smiling, as much as to say that Astrid knew nothing about it. 'And Liv?'

'Oh, I do!' Liv smiled at him. The smile lit her face with great sweetness. Her hair and skin looked extraordinarily and transparently fair in her dark dress. She looked at Sonja and added: 'The arrow is there ... when we need it.'

'Oh, it is there all the time,' Sonja said, 'but we do not always see it.'

'Isn't it the same thing?'

'It is exactly the same thing.'

'There, Olaf!' Liv put her arm on his shoulders, 'you see it is just a miracle ... everything is a miracle.'

'Do you believe in miracles?'

'I believe in everything that happens,' she answered evasively, and went to wash her hands.

'Yes, after it happens.' Astrid turned impishly, her slanting eyes full of merriment.

'And before!' Liv declared, just for the sake of holding her own before the boy. Her mother came and took hold of Aunt Sonja's arm and they went away, and Astrid followed them. 'Wait for me, Olaf?' she pleaded, and the boy waited.

He stood beside her as she washed her hands, twisting the soapy lather off her fingers. 'You can't know before!' he persisted sturdily. She laughed at him, not merrily and hard, like Astrid, but soft, deep laughter, that seemed to stay far down in her bosom, like his mother's. 'That,' she gave the towel a flick, 'is where the miracle comes in!'

As they went downstairs, hand in hand, he told her that he would take her to a place in the forest where, if you stayed ever so still, so still that your breath scarcely came, she would see hares leaping, and sometimes — his voice was full of awe — in the midst of them Hulder, the one who lures young men into the mountains.

Sonja Krag sat at the head of the long supper table in a carved chair with a very high back. The back made a dark panel behind her against the light-coloured wall. High up on the wall were a reindeer's antlers. The windows were shut, but the curtains were not drawn. Against the panes of shining glass, caught between the two lights, the day still clamoured, pleading against the bright candles which burned in branches on the table. In the softening upward light Sonja Krag looked very young — almost as young as Liv. But when you looked from her to Liv you saw that she was not young at all, only very warm and living looking, ripe. Her throat looked so strong and firm rising out of her mauve cloth dress. She wore a red shawl embroidered in blue, and the colours of the shawl and her dress harmonised and sank into each other. As Liv entered the room she saw her aunt's hands grasping the silver servers over the dish of fjeldorret. The servers had flat, intricately woven handles, very old, like silver that had come out of a buried ship, and they rose out of her aunt's hands like oars. Her mother was talking, leaning forward, folding and unfolding her hands on the cloth as she spoke, and recounting many things, one after the other, old things, remembrances, punctuated by short pleas for verification and recognition. She was making a very human effort towards her sister, trying to pick her and herself up where they had left off twenty years ago, and to pick up their husbands and children as well. She was urged on by Sonja's terrible habit of saying nothing. It had always been typical of Sonja to let her run on and on, or stop, as though nothing that she was saying was of any significance. It was part of Sonja's selfishness.

Sonja knew that, as she exhausted herself, she would remember to think that, so she tried to quell the judgement before it rose. It was the merest politeness, and the politeness, it seemed to her, marked the bridge that had arisen between. The space had always been there. But now the bridge of politeness made it possible to carry something from her across it. She accepted it, but she hated herself for being false.

'You are wonderful, Anna, you forget nothing.'

'Yes, yes, you really must come to see us. Let us spend a winter in Oslo together. It is quite wrong of you to shut yourself up here in these mountains, no theatres, nothing.'

Liv, ceasing to listen to Astrid and Olaf, looked up the table and saw a strange expression on her aunt's face. Her aunt's eyes were lowered and her eyelashes seemed to be smiling, lifted at the corners with something wild and sly in them. The wildness and slyness was denied by her mouth, which was sad, terribly sad, and her eyes, when she opened them, had nothing really hidden in them. They were open, some far memory caught in them, and locked. Liv was astonished when her aunt said to her directly, right down the table, as though it was her that she had been brooding upon, 'I hear that you want to travel.'

'Why, yes,' she smiled, warmed, and for the first time feeling encouraged on the subject. She was immediately frozen by her aunt's indifference. Sonja did not look at her. There was a strange bitterness in the way with which her eyes went down again, and the lashes again seemed to glint like a faun's, knowing what they knew and what nobody human ought to know. Liv felt like that about them, felt as if her aunt were not human like that, too cold to be human.

Now why on earth, thought Sonja, turning from the girl's eagerness in a fright, was I fool enough to ask her that. It occurred to her that her will must be going to pieces if she could suddenly, just because of her sister's chatter, and to escape from it, lose control of her intentions. She had decided up there in the bedroom with Anna, never to ask the girl about it, never to begin it, to let Liv tell her herself. It alarmed her to think that her reserves were so fragile that she could at random, and in that manner, betray herself. She withdrew from the girl's hopefulness with a sort of pity and scorn for herself. 'You forget, my dear Anna,' she said in smooth control once more, 'that my life is not a void. Johan needs me....' He depended upon her as the sea depends upon a breakwater, to save him from overdoing it. 'And also my boys. There is always a great deal to do.' These were excuses, but the shade and tone of her voice ratified them and made them serve as reasons.

Liv's courage evaporated and hope went cold again. Her ears again responded to Olaf's voice challenging Astrid, who was bent on teasing him, not taking him seriously, as though that was the proper method to treat a cousin who was, at the same time, a little boy. Then, once more, as if she were a strand being woven from one to the other, her aunt retrieved her again.

'You must tell me about it some time.'

'Yes, Aunt Sonja.' But what else was there to tell? What was the use of telling?

Sonja saw the reserve catch the girl's assent and close it, and she was glad. It absolved her from obligations. It seemed to her quite extraordinary that she should be presiding over a table of women. It accounted, perhaps, for her dislodgement. She had been disarmed by these foreign feminine under-currents of thoughts stored, as it were, in pantries, neat and labelled and knowing, as Anna always knew, what they were made for. She wished that Johan had not had to go away and take Erik with him. Erik would have been a help. He'd have kept that lively Japanese child, Astrid, off Olaf. She had one of those sharp pangs of misery when she hated any of her brood being absent, cut off; when she wished that high-schools had never been invented, and that the young could be educated somewhere near enough for a mother to look on. She saw Georges and Bernt sitting in their vacant places and Tore — where Liv was — at the end of the table where the daylight still came, and was stopped by the candles. She wondered what was happening to them — were they in bed and safely asleep, was Tore dreaming of his old friend, Balder? They had only, it seemed to her, been a very few years with her. Erik had come back. He would always, more or less, even if he married, be there, for Johan had taken him into partnership. He was the one she liked least of all her sons. He had been born before she had begun to love her husband. Soon they would take Olaf too, change him. The thought of losing him in any way, even for the brief period of schooling, was so unbearable that it made her speak to him, gain his attention. 'Have you converted her yet?'

'Oh, she's quite hopeless ... you are, you know!' he added to Astrid, and scored against her.

And Liv thought, weaving the voices again in a ribbon that trailed far away, out of reach: 'I shall tell her. I shall tell her after all. She is like a queen, sitting there in the high-backed chair, a white-headed queen. She has a queen's beauty. She ought to have a crown.' She looked where the crown ought to have been and saw the deer's antlers duplicated in shadow on the wall above, pleated with the shadow, like the thorns in the crucifixion crowns in her father's collection. She remembered her father's long frail fingers on the ebony crosses, holding them up for her to see, shakily and tremblingly. Gradually she felt her blood grow hot and rush through her. She heard her mother telling Aunt Sonja that she was going to marry Harald Christensen. She felt so distressed with shame that she closed her eyes and held them so until she could bear them closed no longer, and then opened them just a little, painfully, upon the spinning disc of the plate in front of her. She said 'Yes, yes,' to something without knowing what it was. Astrid's laughter pealed, a perfect mock of bells, against her ears. It made it possible for her to raise her eyes and stare, full of bitter scorn, at her sister.

She made up for it later in the bedroom, lying in the deep bed waiting for Astrid to come in. Astrid never meant to cut her into pieces like that. There was no use in blaming her. She remembered her aunt's napery, the silver swimming on the white cloth (the glide into the sheets had brought it back to her) so she said, wiping her anger away: 'Aunt Sonja has lovely linen!'

'Heavenly!' said Astrid, putting the scissors back into the manicure box, 'and have you noticed how she does her monograms ... three letters; she's put the J for Johan in between the S and K.'

Liv had noticed. Something in her mind declared: she worked those after her marriage.

'Isn't it a funny house, Liv? Bare, dreadfully ... after ours.'

'Very!' She liked it. It had its own beauty, a beauty beyond all laws like her aunt's. Fashions had nothing at all to do with it. It had grown together. It was big and gracious and used, nothing clashed. You went from room to room, and it was like going from member to member of the same family — furniture was older or younger, the walls older or younger — that was all, but the same atmosphere, the same traces of the same family, the same carved horns and hunter's tassels, the same deep frames, the same absence of trifles, and stacks of queer things, like the fishing-rods in the gang cupboard, and the rows and rows of male boots in the corners. Astrid's skin looked very brown against her white nightdress. It was odd that she never went brown, like Astrid. The blue bows on Astrid's hair made a small child of her again, as she was when she was at that school in Oslo. 'Aren't you coming to bed?' she asked.

'Of course I am, when I've finished. I'm not like you!' Liv always brushed her teeth and her hair, and positively jumped out of her clothes.

She laughed her low deep laugh out of the bedclothes.

'We aren't all good looking and engaged to be married.'

Liv sat up. 'Don't, Astrid, don't! If you knew how I hated it. I don't feel … engaged to be married.' She blazed to a sudden full blame of herself. 'I took his ring, but I was honest, I told him … I took his ring because, because…' she could not bring herself to say that she had a feeling that Fru Christensen wanted her to take it … not to hurt him. 'I couldn't hurt him. I had to take it. I wish, I wish I could go away so that he could forget me. I want to go away.'

Astrid turned and regarded her, seriously, sympathetically. 'It's a pity you can't … you could go with Barbra Grondahl — to Paris. I should prefer to go to England. The English, Liv! The nice, tall Englishmen!' Astrid's English was better than her French.

Liv was thinking that she could not go back to Odda to cheat Harald Christensen. Whatever she did she could not do that. Her mother wanted her to marry Harald, it was all ready and arranged in her mother's mind that she should marry Harald and live in Mornesund. She decided then to tell her aunt, to tell her the whole story and ask her to help her. She said aloud: 'I like Aunt Sonja.'

'Anybody can see that you do!' Astrid pulled back the clothes and began to snuggle into the bed. 'She's rather ... superior ... she makes me feel that I'm no bigger than Olaf!'

'Oh, no...' Liv hesitated. There was nothing in Astrid that matched Aunt Sonja.

Then the next morning, when she went downstairs and found her aunt surrounded by her men folk, who had returned before any of them were out of bed, and by Olaf, and two maids to whom she was giving directions, she felt that Astrid was right. Her aunt was very, very remote, and she was only a little speck in the beam of her interests. She was bestowing what looked exactly like encouragement upon the bearded man who was evidently Uncle Johan, and at the same time she was undoing the buttons on Olaf's tunic and buttoning them again — he had done them all wrong — and she was giving instructions to the girl Hilde about the breakfast and saying directly (it sounded to Liv practically at the same time, as though she had two voices) to the other girl: 'Give the note to Tella.' Her greeting to Liv was as fleeting as the glance of a bird in flight. It was Uncle Johan who really noticed her, putting out his hand:

'Which one are you?'

'Liv,' she looked at her aunt as though the short word needed substantiation.

'No!' He refused to believe it. 'Sonja! Sonja!' He put his arm round her and pulled her round to face Aunt Sonja, who had to stop to look at her. 'She ought to be yours,' he said, and Aunt Sonja ceased suddenly to split and divide herself and became single, with something concentrated and sad in her expression. It made Liv wonder what had she done. It was like penitence.

'I saw it at once, Johan. I saw myself as a girl, especially,' she addressed Liv, 'when you were sitting on the bed last night beside Olaf.' She had wished then that the girl had been her daughter. She had always wanted a daughter. It was too late now. Olaf had come seven years after Bernt. He was the last. She seemed to fail, at that moment, before her husband — not for him but for herself, and she beheld herself, at Liv's age. It was a prodigal age, the age of giving. One should never mourn for gifts bestowed. No! No! It wasn't that, but that she hated waste, not because she was mean, but because she was too intensely aware of the treasures of life. She remembered Liv's flush at the supper table and she felt assured that this girl would never squander her values. It made her proud of her, proud as she might have been of the pride in her own daughter. 'And this,' she said, feeling Erik's discomfort at her elbow, 'is your cousin Erik.'

For two days Aunt Sonja remained like this, distant and absorbed. It was impossible to penetrate to her. There was no approach. The contacts in the house and garden were like street meetings, purely casual and always on the way to some-thing else. It was only through Olaf that she came near her. The boy saved her from severance, for through him, she felt the glow and life-giving wonder of her aunt's temperament — the tranquillity that was as a core of poetry, transfusing her with an intimacy that resembled clairvoyance, hiding nothing. The boy so loved and believed in her that his simplest word about her seemed to clap cymbals above her meaning. To Liv, dwelling in the old house that was so stamped with their inhabitation, it seemed that the music of the boy's devotion ran everywhere, touching everything within and without with the proof that a woman lived there who loved much. She drew from the boy the reflection of what he drew from his mother. It brought peace. She was quiet in her aunt's house, waiting. But she did not know what she was waiting for. Trifles became potent to her, powerful as the stars that make their tiny eyelets into heaven, promising the vision of a paradise that was yet to come.

Sonja was keenly aware of the girl's presence in the house. She knew that she had power to influence her, and just because it was there, unsought, she refrained from using it. She hated to use it. She was lost in this sense of power. It was continually being drawn from her in the guidance of her sons, in Johan's dependence on her. Outside his business affairs life seemed to bereave him. It was she who pulled the threads of his desertion together and knotted them for him so that they became strong and useful, something that would support him in shipwreck. She always hoped that he would be the first to die, for he would be pitiful without her. And to the boys she knew that she gave what no other woman would ever have the power to give them. She had borne and nursed them and supported them, been so great with them that they had been able to lie back and swing in her love (in all that was included in her love) and let the world go by. Never with any other woman would they be able to do that without letting the woman go by as well, whereas she — she remained. She was always there. The patches she mended, the buttons she sewed on, the bread she baked, were mere signs on the invisible truth. There she was, like the pillars of society, holding up her world ... holding it up while they wanted her. They would always want her — in the end as in the beginning. It was terrible to her to imagine it. There were times when, owing to natural fatigue or spiritual exhaustion, she felt so inadequate that the whole edifice of the life that surrounded her became fragile as a bubble which any fool could blow to pieces. There were times when she wished human beings could be born ripe with all earthly experiences from the brows of God — like the heroes of old who took seven-league steps across the mountains. Great men. Little mountains. But the mountains of the world were very high and mighty, mankind went astray on them. They were forlorn and lost because they were no longer born greater than the mountains. She loved the grand purifying mountains. She would have liked to live on the very top of Stortoppen. Years ago, before the birth of her second son, she had pretended to go to visit friends, and she had gone up on the crest of Stortoppen....

She thought of that day when, at the end of their first week, Johan took them all in his great car to picnic there. It was quite an affair taking enough food for all of them and packing them and the food into the car. (On that day years ago she had taken a dry loaf with her and had quenched her thirst in a spring, frugal as a pilgrim. She believed that every human life had, at least, its one day of pilgrimage — the humility at the end of the journey.) Anna and she sat side by side with Olaf between them and opposite sat Liv and Astrid. Liv's knees were touching hers. They were each conscious of their intimacy and nearness. Liv wished that the others weren't there, so that she and her aunt could have driven together along the edge of the beautiful forest. The pines shook their plumy crests into an air that was blue as the sky itself. The trunks spread in great serried ranks, bronze and purple, glittering with mystic patterns as they passed. They rose as from some vulcan's furnace on the edge of the world, magical and fecund symbols of a source that seemed likely to last longer than anything on earth itself. And down below them the valley lay in the web of the morning. 'Isn't it a lovely world?' she said to Aunt Sonja, and Aunt Sonja smiled and leaned forward to her and Astrid.

'Do you know, Johan says that the ark was a Norse ship and Noah a Viking, and that these crests were the first that showed when the waters began to go down.'

'And the dove lit on them,' chimed in Olaf.

'But we haven't got all the two and two animals in Norway,' argued Astrid.

'Trust Astrid to be practical,' said her mother, 'to tell the truth.' She disapproved of Sonja's passion for fairy tales, of what she called — nodding in Olaf's direction — stuffing the child with shams.

Sonja pretended not to hear. Anna's sense of truth and hers were not the same. She kept the smile on her face a second longer than it wanted to stay, and then let it go. It was true, of course, he was getting too old for fairy tales. But he loved them and she loved them. It was a lovely world, where everything came out as you wished; where, when you grew tired of the expected, you could twist it into freakishness such as the princess became a guinea-pig and had no tail which was a great humiliation, and if you objected to the humiliation, you could endow her bite with a special poison which made her omnipotent amongst guinea-pigs, and so puissant that thrones and dynasties tumbled down like tea-cups when she nibbled laburnum peas or ate a worm. She and Olaf enjoyed themselves thoroughly in that kingdom. 'But only the fairy tales are really true,' she found herself saying, and looking at Liv.

'She believes in nothing real,' Liv thought, 'or she wouldn't say that.' She asked, after a pause: 'Is it, Aunt Sonja, when we believe in things...' she searched, '...oh, things like railways and aeroplanes, that we begin not to want fairy tales? I've never,' she explained, 'wanted them ... never like you and Olaf.'

'What did you want ... railways and aeroplanes?'

'No ... everything to be real.'

Poor child, Sonja thought, and said nothing. She and Liv did not speak to each other again until, together, they found themselves unpacking the luncheon which Erik and Johan had carried up from the last stretch of road. Johan had gone back to the car to inspect it, something had gone wrong, and Erik had gone off with Astrid to get kindling-wood to make a fire. Liv thought it was such a clever and compact idea to pack the lunch in a trunk. 'I've never heard of a picnic packed into a cabin trunk.'

'But it's the only way to do it,' Sonja said briskly, 'it's such a good trunk for the purpose, with a tin lining.' She was trying to remember which sandwiches there were least of and had to be served first. 'It's a trunk Johan took with him to the East Indies.'

'Uncle Johan has been to the East Indies?' Liv was surprised.

'Oh, yes, he was the "one" in his family!'

'The "one" in his family?'

'Yes, the "one". Isn't there always one who travels, one with the Viking's itch, amongst us Norwegians? Tore had it. You must know that?'

'Yes, I know. At least, I know when you put it like that, I...' she straightened her back and paused with the pile of plates in her hand, 'I've got it, Aunt Sonja! But Father would never let me ... and Mother won't.'

Chapter Two

Sonja could have bitten her tongue. It was thinking of those sandwiches. She had precipitated what she had been avoiding. She had begun to hope that Liv would never tell her this. She felt that she ought to say to her instantly: 'Don't go. Stay where you are, you'll be happier.' She would fulfil in this manner some remote loyalty to Anna. But would she be happier? Was Anna happier? You could not, she knew down to the base of her being, set happiness in a mould and turn it out like a pudding. Loyalty to Anna was a dunce's way of putting it. Liv waited, denied by her silence. She bent her head and went on with the unpacking. They were alone, Sonja rejoiced, she and Liv on the wild, desolate mountain, on her beloved Stortoppen. It seemed to her that they were together on the crown of the earth, and that if they died and were buried there the sun would come down upon them and lick them up into his flames, a true cremation. The tiny orange and purple flowers around them were washed and clean, and minute as fresh embroidery. The heather was soft like velvet, and so were the gleams of blue-berries under their polished leaves. She always wondered how the blue-berries came to be there, and imagined that Bacchus had wandered up here for his last revel and shed his wreath for seed before he danced his last wild dance into the chasm of eternity.

Liv hated her for her silence. Astrid was right, as usual. She was too aloof to understand, to care enough for comprehension. It roused her dignity, and made her say with quite an air of having carried the matter about in a pair of scales for years, 'Well, I have considered it, and considered it, and the more I try to give it up, the wish, I mean, the more I go on wishing ... wishing....'

'Wishing for what, Liv?'

'To live, Aunt Sonja ... to see the world!'

'Look at what there is of it here, my child, it is quite magnificent.' It wasn't really the world, here, in this solitude, certainly not the life which the girl meant by the world. This was more like eternity ... space, and the sky so close that you had only to reach up your hand to touch the sun and moon and stars.

Liv laughed at her. 'This,' she said, putting the roast chicken out on the heather, 'is just a dream, a dream! Don't you feel it? It would be all right if I were a bird,' she pointed to one in flight, 'it would be almost heaven then!'

'And you don't want heaven?'

'On this earth!'

It was Sonja's turn to laugh. 'I can see,' she said steadily, 'that you are quite likely to get it.'

'How?' Liv stared at her and waited.

'Because you know what it is.'

Liv pondered before she spoke. 'But I don't know. I only know what it isn't.'

'It's the same thing, Liv.'

'But is it?' she demanded, after a pause.

Sonja had spread the cloth and was putting the sandwiches out of their wrappings. She hated picnics and always tried to make them appear as little like picnics as possible. 'It means,' she said from some far away realm of logic in her mind, for she was really wondering at that moment at what stage of the repast they would begin to feel cramped, and if she ought to take the cloth up again and lay it over by some stones on which she and Anna could sit. The younger ones wouldn't mind so much '... that you will find out your mistakes.'

'Doesn't everybody?'

'No, Liv,' she answered giving the girl full attention at last, as if there would never be another opportunity, 'some people do not even know when they have made them.'

'But how can I be sure not to make mistakes. I can't!'

'Of course not.' She saw desire, misty with longing, fill the girl's eyes, and gave her sympathy in silence.

It was to Liv, as if a beam passed through them both, uniting them across an abyss of human errors. She pleaded: 'Even if it is wrong, Aunt Sonja, I want to go. I want to find out. They all want me to marry Harald Christensen....'

'Do you not love him?'

'Yes ... but ... what is love?'

'Is that what you want to find out?' She understood, as in a flash, that the girl needed the separation that creates understanding. It was necessary to her, not a wild longing that you could turn into any stray usefulness. It had been quite different in her own case. Johan had not been there — until she came back. It changed everything, the boy Harald Christensen being there. She saw Liv, like a brave little ship, anchored in the seas of her travels by this entanglement with Harald Christensen.

'Yes ... and other things, too.'

'But you are truly engaged to him?'

'I suppose so.... Look!' She held up the hand with Fru Christensen's ring upon it. Sharp, as though it had been cut out of her consciousness with a pair of scissors, she remembered Fru Christensen's presence. 'I could not, something would not let me, refuse.'

'Ah!' sighed Aunt Sonja, 'that is a little like Fate!'

'Fate!' The word filled her with terror. It was so fraught with defeat, with power so insistent that nothing you could do could ever alter or control it. Fate, it seemed to her, was deep and hidden as the seeds of death: the death that had taken her father, that would ultimately take each one of them. She shivered. And again she remembered Fru Christensen standing in the station, watching Harald fastening hers and Astrid's skis on to the train. The skis shone on the train like a sheath of spears. The snow was white on the heights and valleys, and the cores of the trees burned black under the white burden. The evergreen trees were darkest green, like water sprung under green shadows. Fru Christensen had stood there, watching her son, and smiling, and at the last moment she had said, still smiling, that she did not feel well enough to come with them. Harald was frightfully cross about it, but she did not mind, she even seemed pleased that he could be so cross, because she wasn't going with them. She insisted on his going without her, and she had commended him to Liv, saying, 'Take care! Do not get buried, either of you!' That was the very last time that she had seen Fru Christensen standing in the snow. 'I do not want to be engaged to him.'

'No,' Sonja said it absently. She had the feeling that she had to tell Liv what to do. It seemed to her that the conviction blew through her, like the fine, exhilarating air of the mountain, chasing doubt. Anna gave the girl nothing but opposition, and to give opposition to the young was like giving good counsel to an idiot. It was of no use to him, it did not touch nor ameliorate his special anguish. She felt also that she owed something to Liv as well as to Anna. She thought of the girl as her own daughter — craving to go. And she thought instantly: but I'd go with her. Anna would never be persuaded to go, for Anna dreaded strange tongues and peoples. And then — supposing she were her daughter — it did not follow that she would want her mother to go with her. Well, it was out of the question. Liv was *not* her daughter, and nothing was to be served by taking up false attitudes. Here she was, wanting so very badly to go, to take flight. She, at Liv's age, had known that heartache. Long, long ago, when she was younger than Liv, she had gone. She had gone to Paris to study music. She remembered perfectly everything that had happened to her there ... the little grey streets ... the end! Dear God, she would wish no girl, least of all a girl such as Liv, to suffer as she had suffered.... She took her thoughts firmly and deafened them, silenced them, thought of Olaf, thought of Erik as a baby on her lap — fastening the binder over his little fat belly, thought of the umbrella she had lost the day she went to Trondjem with Tore, the colour of the labels on the picnic trunk, the sun in Liv's hair before she said wildly: 'Oh, Liv, what am I to do with you ... tell you to go?' No, no, no! She hadn't said it, only thought and said it to herself. Liv had not heard. They ought not to have let her go. They! Oh, the poor They! Nobody could have stopped her. She was demented with longing. She was like the Newfoundland bitch that had gone on board at Archangel and would not be put off, and come to Trondjem and bestowed her litter on a poor ostler who had given her shelter. It was fate. The human will had nothing to do with it. It was like following the star of the Magi ... it led to Calvary. Liv could no more be put off than she had been. They had trusted her. She had trusted herself. Well, she had carried off the trust. She sometimes felt that regret was the greatest of weaknesses, especially in women. Men over-reached themselves, but men recovered. Oh, yes, recovered, battling in streams of failures, in floods, in torrents of failures. It accounted for their brotherhood. They knew what it was to go under. It was only women who stood like peeled and blazing white trees in the rivers, letting the waters swirl.... 'Once,' she began to speak quickly, before the others came back, 'I felt just like you, as though I'd break my heart to go ... didn't scratch the Viking out of me. I went....' Truly, she was caught, she couldn't even put it plainly.

'Did you regret it?'

The short, sharp question stabbed her into sense. 'I ... I did not like it.' That was a lie, a mortal lie. She had said it to mislead, to warn her.

'Why, Aunt Sonja?'

'Don't ask questions, child,' she retorted in her mind. The girl's face was so lovely, with those dark lakes of eyes under the level brows. Her fair, crisp hair was blowing in little tendrils on her temples, curls just like a cherub's. She was so innocent, so very innocent ... and yet so strong, as though the innocence would always remain. She had a passionate, sweet mouth, and then, before you knew where you were with her, it went quite sullen with determination. She was not quite sure of the full worth of innocence, but she herself, being a mother, would never be the first to break it. She rallied the clairvoyance, the mountain-sense that had got into her head. 'You see, Liv, it depends upon how you take ... if you fall in love, for instance....'

'Isn't that a proof that I am not meant to marry Harald Christensen?'

'You must never forget, never forget for one moment, that Harald Christensen is there.'

The thunder mounted from Liv's mouth to her brows. 'I am not likely to forget that.' The young voice was sarcastic.

'There,' reasoned Sonja, 'I'm making a muddle of it. I mean that you must never let yourself want to forget it.'

'But how can I?'

'Ah!' she shrugged her shoulders, and her hand swept out and back again to the pot of jelly that she was opening. 'I do not mean anything, don't misunderstand, dishonourable, but...' she saw Anna coming through the heather, holding Olaf's hand, '... oh, Liv darling! Something so overwhelming may happen to you so that you won't know what you are doing!'

'I don't think,' said Liv, with the thunder now in her voice, 'that I shall go so mad as that!'

'Well ... I did!' She flung reserve to the winds, reserve and pride out on the air, knowing that the presence of those who were approaching would catch them like a wall and throw them back to her in time for her to catch them and take them again into her keeping. She knew that Liv would never tell, never speak of this to a living soul. She put out her hand, making a plea of the gesture. 'You see, Liv, I know what I am talking about.' It was as though she had said: 'And I, also, I am no fool.'

Liv sat back on her heels, limp, rebelling because her mother and Olaf and Erik and Astrid were coming towards them. She was humiliated before her aunt, yet warmed by the strangest pity. She had suffered. You could see that she had suffered. It accounted for that queer, forbidding sadness that came into her face, and froze you from her, away, because you could not follow. It made her cry out, lowering and deepening her tones so that they sounded oddly passionate in that wild and vast place. 'Oh, Aunt Sonja! I *do* believe in you!'

Sonja was trapped by the tightness of her throat, the scald of tears that did not rise to the shedding, and she, like Liv, felt humiliated and torn, as if she had been pardoned. She, who had never asked absolution from a living soul. It was, she believed, nothing more or less than, standing before the younger generation — being stripped and understood — and, was it? — pitied! She looked into the distance to where the clarity of the air met cloud and became mist, edging to purple, as though it drew the earth along with it as a halo, changing the sky to shade. It was beautiful here on her beloved mountain where, for the second time, she had revealed her soul. I shall come a third time, she reckoned, smiling secretly, making an assignation of it. I shall come again. 'We must,' she said, aware that they had accomplished nothing, 'speak of this again.'

Liv turned suddenly childish about it, restrained probably by the approaching figures. 'Thank you so much, Aunt Sonja, thank you!'

'For what?' she demanded sharply.

'Because you have helped me to make up my mind.'

Olaf's arms were full of tiny purple-headed flowers. He called out; 'We thieved them from Nisse!'

'Goats like old men!' gasped Fru Evensen, across the short space. 'The funniest goats I've ever seen!' She was very hot and tired with the climb up from the car. She had thrown back her cloak and her stomach stuck out under her black dress.

Sonja felt very cool and young, as young as Liv. Her eyes drank in the joy on Olaf's face and went dark with the glory. 'Come here, my son!' She held out the white apron that she had tied on over her coat and he emptied in the armful of tiny, salt-scented blossoms. The world seemed to spin under the clouds, very great and strong, and with a speed that was like music, edged and swished by the lullaby of the trees at the end of the earth.

Liv felt it, too. Her aunt's change communicated itself to her as if, in that brief interval, they had established a common language. They were all suddenly happy, free, and in harmony — her mother, hot and tired, watching Olaf spill the flowers in a purple fall into his mother's apron, and Erik and Astrid rising breast high over the hill of heather.

A sharp exaltation shot through Liv. She put out her hands and cried to Olaf, sharing in some recess of her senses the love that was exchanged between him and Sonja: 'Come!' she cried, 'I'll give you a good whirl!' and, catching the hands he immediately extended to her and placing their toes together, they swung round and round until they flew asunder and tottered into the scratching bushes that surrounded them. Their laughter rose out of the heather like a flock of birds. 'My, that was good!' she called to him where he was buried, 'wasn't it?'

'Oh, oh!' he gurgled. 'I'm blinded with dizziness!'

She got up, not dizzily like he, for it was she who had swung him, but tottering with the spirit of the thing and offered to do it again with Astrid, so Astrid and she swung and swung and tumbled, and then Erik and Astrid did it, then Astrid and Olaf, and their spirits mounted with the wildness, intoxicating them so that they were whirled like insects, like bees, into an ecstasy, until Sonja said, not breaking in upon them, but arriving at the end of her preparations:

'One of you might run down and fetch Johan!' It was Erik who, panting from the pull with Astrid, from the force of holding against her so that he should be the swinger, cried, lining them up: 'One, two, three … and away!' and off they all ran, helter skelter together.

'What a troop!' Sonja exclaimed, a pack of youth! It was lovely watching them, feeling how young they were, so safe and untried; Liv, taller than any of them, something gentle about her form and movements that made her lose against the others. Olaf raced better than any of them — a boy's race, utterly flexible and fleet. She thought of the youths in the Olympic games, some mother's heart catching with the break and beauty of victory. The moment repeated itself from generation to generation, falling where it wished — amongst the crowds, amongst the public games, in any garden, and here so completely for her own eyes upon the heights of Stortoppen. She held her laced fingers across her breast, pressing the sweetness there to the heart's memory. They disappeared. She turned slowly, to Anna, her eyes very darkened and still smiling. 'You know,' she said, 'we can't do much with them, can we? They belong so entirely to themselves, they stretch so far beyond us, Anna. What can we do but look on?'

Anna had raked no classic memory. Her mind never had these indulgences, and besides she was too hot. She wanted to be cool more than anything else. She said tartly: 'I think we do a great deal for them. Where would they be without us?'

Sonja made a seat for her. 'They wouldn't be born, they wouldn't be alive.... They'd have perished long ago of measles and other immature maladies if they had been left to themselves, abandoned like Moses in a bulrush. And seeing, Anna, that we've done that to them, given them birth, we can never get out of their debt!'

'That,' said Anna, 'I feel is quite a wrong attitude. We can, we do, quite a lot for them, we are always preserving them, preventing them....'

'That's just it,' Sonja interrupted. 'Do we? Were *we* prevented? And is it always best to be prevented, to be thwarted?' Anna had no sons to deal with; she might not be able to understand what she was trying to say. Anna had married a clergyman; she was so terribly accustomed to the ten commandments that she wore them as a model for every-thing. She believed in the ten commandments and had nothing against them. They had the full Hebraic gesture of a man — in the time when humanity went in herds, like buffaloes — saying 'thou shalt nots' to men who were only beginning to establish records in human behaviour? Humanity, one had to admit it, began very badly, and the badness was still running. But when you dealt with it only in the Hebraic terms, in the terms of the man smiting the air right and left with the force of tribal must-nots, you left a great deal to be accounted for. There were shades and shades of wisdom. There was a foresight that was completely excluded from obedience to parents. 'You know, Anna, I never feel like that — that it is possible to keep them always....' She spread out her hand with the five fingers clustered downward: 'Where you can touch them, feel what is going on inside them.' She saw the heads of her five sons under her fingers, like the pigmies running under Gulliver, making a monster of her. 'They are never, at any time, on our level, nor are we on theirs.'

'They are another generation. I admit that, Sonja, but we, at least, know much that they do not know. We can see where they are going to ... if we take care, I mean!'

She was silent, staring out, feeling out that it was no use trying to explain to Anna, because Anna only knew what she wanted to know. Far down in the valley, to the east of where they were sitting, she saw a red butterfly, poised out of dense trees. It was her home. In that house, cut off for miles from any other habitation, she had gathered her life into its present form. She thought of days there, episodes, of going upstairs to her first childbirth and seeing the snow so thick on the window ledges that the bedroom was dark as a stable. She would die there. She would be buried in the mountain graveyard. A road wound through the valley, upwards, zig-zagged as a flash of lightning, forking its way through pasture and forest. If it were really true what Anna had said then you would be able to produce human types to order, you would be able to take them up like a box of dolls, and shake them out according to costume, princess or peasant, tinker or tailor, fully priced and ready to hand on to the young of the next generation. No it wasn't like that. 'It isn't really true,' she said dreamily, watching the red butterfly still rising from the trees.

'Sometimes, Sonja, you really exasperate me.'

'I don't mean to,' she smiled. 'It's having only boys, perhaps, I can't feel like that, that you can map out their futures, we can see that they are properly fed and clothed, and, of course, educated.' She had her doubts about the education. There were such things as mathematics and chemistry, etc., but there were other things that no organised effort could put into you and plant deep — like the things that had gone down and seeded in her own soul. Those things came only from experience, and she was too much of a woman to underrate them. Johan came over the crest of the dwarf birches, an arm round Liv and an arm round Astrid, drawing them up with them, with Erik and Olaf pulling at the ends. They were singing, chanting a chorus. They ought to be naked, she thought, with wreaths in their hair and garlands round their waists. She waved to them. They did not break the line to wave back to her, but their voices rose and swelled towards her. Liv was leaning towards Johan, taking more support from him. She looked suddenly at Anna and said: 'Liv has been telling me about her great wish to travel.'

'Yes, yes! What did you say, Sonja, tell me?' Anna was nervous, and regarding her pleadingly, all the determination, the knowing-everything gone out of her.

'Nothing ... yet.' She stooped and straightened the knife and fork at her feet. 'If I were you, I'd let her go. She is not in love with that Christensen boy.'

'That's just it....'

'But don't you see,' she asked quietly, 'if you force her to marry him she'll run away?'

'No, Sonja. You can't think that!'

'I do. She doesn't know where she is. I should say that she is where she was when she was about fifteen. What is the use of keeping her like that? You won't keep her; you'll lose her!'

'And do you think that if I let her go she'd ... she'd come back and marry Harald Christensen?'

'She'd come back....'

They had all come back. Johan was holding out begrimed hands to her, making her feel what an idiot she was to have forgotten to bring soap.

'What am I to do with them?' he asked, standing there like a baby, expecting to have them wiped for him.

'Scratch in the earth like a badger,' she answered, and away he went and scratched in the earth like a badger. Astrid laughed at him, and he threatened to wash her, too, with the same method. He looked very young, full of strength and vigour, looking up as he stooped, at her, teasing her, flirting with her. Sonja realised, and saw him suddenly away from her, treating every young woman like that. Men could always be lovers. She shouted to him: 'I brought a towel!' and recalled that she had stuffed it into the hood of the car! It was down there, half a mile from them, making a mock of her because she hated picnics and took the oddest precautions and provisions against just these sorts of things. Johan carried the teasing, very chivalrously, she thought, from Astrid to her, telling her that the towel was standing up now, unfurling itself into a white flag of appeal for those who were not born to picnic. 'No,' she agreed that picnics did not count for much in her destiny, and was pulled up sharp as a blow by Anna's voice saying, as though she had caught her out in some sort of deceit, to Liv:

'I hear that you have enlisted your aunt's sympathy!'

Oh, that wasn't fair. It made her feel as though she had deceived Liv. 'Well, not quite that,' she said, stopping Anna before she said worse. 'Neither I nor Liv could tell you how it happened. We simply began to talk.' She remembered:

───────── Chapter Two ─────────

'Oh, it was Johan's trunk that did it; it began with Johan's trunk!'

'Come here, trunk!' Johan whistled to it as though it was a dog, and even Anna laughed.

'And your going to the East Indies.' Liv endeavoured to make it clearer to him.

'I simply,' he had to explain, 'do not understand a word of what you are talking about!'

And Erik contributed:

'"Oh, tell me quick," the traveller said,

"I'm tired and want to go to bed!"'

Sonja rescued the affair, lifting it by the scruff of the neck like a drowning animal and shaking it quite clear upon all of them.

'It's Liv. She wants to make the grand tour instead of getting married!'

Uncle Johan squatted before the roast chickens, seized the carving knife and flourished it. 'Why not,' he said, terrifying Anna, 'do both?'

It seemed to Liv that it was she and not the chicken that was on the dish, being cut up there before their eyes: the piece that was to marry Harald Christensen, the piece that wanted to go to Paris, and the piece that had told Aunt Sonja. She did not dare to look at any of them, but she was conscious of Erik's criticism, of his sitting opposite, cross-legged, watching her with the green eyes that were peculiarly his own under his mother's eyebrows — the exact image of Aunt Sonja's — and his father's mouth pursed, firmly shut, and somehow not quite serious, and the crackling white, oddly pure, square of the napkin tucked under his collar into the V-opening of his pull-over.

'Don't go, Liv. It's nicer here!' Olaf pleaded, and everybody seemed to laugh at once.

'Out of the mouth of babes!' said Anna Evensen, holding her plate for Johan to take back a piece of chicken.

Sonja felt the girl's misery. Anna might have waited. It was too bad of her to cast this blight upon the picnic, which was uncomfortable enough, goodness knows, with all of them eating on their knees. She was wondering, searching her wits for something to say that would change the subject, and at the same time not sound too much like drawing the attention of the small child in the dentist's chair to the dicky bird on the ceiling. Then, before she knew where she was, Liv sprang to her feet and fled from them. She took in the flight of the girl's form, the consternation that ran like a shadow through the circle of faces, taking the light out of them. 'Anna! Anna! You shouldn't ... there was no enlistment about it.'

'It is easy,' Anna burst out, 'for you. She isn't your daughter! I know...' she cast her exasperation upon Johan, 'with her looks ... of course it is madness to let her go!'

'If she isn't a fool — and she is not, you know — there's nothing in it.'

Sonja saw that Johan was much more concerned with the satisfaction of his food, his mouth was full, than with the problem of Liv's grand tour. He looked so happy — the happiness deeply embedded in him — as he answered Anna. His eyes glowed ruminantly, purely like a healthy animal's. He waved a fork into the air and declared, addressing them, and in some remote way inveighing against the timidity of women, 'don't make a fuss, don't fuss!' and it seemed to Sonja that his voice carried on secretly into each of their ears: 'Eat, enjoy your food, don't spoil your appetites for a trifle like that!' It was all very well, nobody was making a fuss, for Anna's outburst had to be balanced against her usual way of taking everything, but it was quite distressing to have Liv going off like that.... She wanted to go after her, to send Olaf, and she continued to sit there balancing her plate on her knee. She said: 'It is a pity to spoil the picnic...' and then, there was Liv coming back of her own accord, her head held high, as if nothing had happened. Sonja's reason cried out inside the box of her brain: 'Now watch! What she does now will tell you what she is,' and she remembered at the same time the tiny sting of disappointment she had suffered when Liv had said: 'Thank you, Aunt Sonja,' just because the others were coming. She had said it so tamely, hushing up all the liberties that they had reached to each other.

Liv was in a white-hot rage against herself. But it *had* been unbearable, stripping her before them all as before a judgement. It had happened so suddenly, and just when they were all feeling so hungry, up in that biting air. It was like a flagellation to her, coming as it did after that wonderful moment with her aunt. It spoiled everything for her. She had to run. And as soon as she was out of sight, she had paused, taken in the vast sweeping loveliness of the valley, washing herself in the loveliness, and she became conscious, as by revelation, that the best thing in the world had happened to her. Aunt Sonja was there! Before Aunt Sonja she had no right to falter. It was then that the anger against her mother ran out, and became hot and hotter against herself. She went back.

'Forgive me,' she said directly and clear to her aunt (it was her aunt's picnic), and then to everybody else, 'for making such a fool of myself, but you know,' she sat down again opposite Erik, and looked at him as though he held the verdict, 'I've wanted this so much for years, to go abroad, that I couldn't bear to hear anybody say it was wrong.' She took her eyes from Erik and placed them where her thoughts were — on her mother. 'There, mother! I can't help it, I can't get it out of me, I want to go. I feel now that I must go, even if I have to run away to do it ... and you wouldn't like that!'

Anna's expression filled with dereliction. That was what Sonja had said: 'She'll run away!' She could do it. Her father had left her enough money. Sonja had said, too: 'She'll come back....'

Sonja had a queer glow in her heart. She did not look at Liv, do anything that would embarrass the girl's own clarity of purpose. She believed in her. She would have liked to have said: 'I believe in you,' as Liv had so naïvely but so really said to her. The belief ran between them, and was as sure as courage. She felt her hand, which stayed quite still, poising the knife on her plate, go out and touch Liv's hand and press her arm with that assurance which she was wishing to give her openly and was compelled to hide.

'If you really feel so unhappy about it, Liv, we must see what can be done. Perhaps after your marriage.'

'No!' answered Liv, straight from that divination that had enveloped her, looking upon the valley, 'it must be before my marriage, before.'

Erik's body jerked back from her, as if the shock of her determination were frightening him. A slow mischievous smile spread over Astrid's face. She looked shyly, trying to control it, at Uncle Johan, and Uncle Johan nodded at her, with the air of

one admonishing her to listen. 'Listen to that now,' he seemed
to be saying to her, and she listened. And then, quite abruptly,
flicking his napkin off his chest, he descended upon Liv: 'But
what, my dear girl, do you want to do? Do you want to go
from place to place until you get tired of it, or do you want
to go to one place, and ... oh, do something, get something
out of it? If we all said to you, now, this moment, "Well, go!
Go, my girl, and God bless you," what would you do?'

'I'd go!' She made a triumph of it, smiling radiantly, the
beams of the divination transfiguring her.

'She wants,' said Astrid, in order to help Uncle Johan,
because he had nodded at her when she had not been able to
stop smiling, 'to go to Paris!'

'To do what?'

'That's just it.' Anna seized upon the question like a
weapon and brandished it in defence of *her* principles. 'She
doesn't know.'

'I might,' said Liv — the inspiration lasting wonderfully —
'if I am going to be married, take up cooking!' She had never
given the idea of cooking a moment's thought. It was exactly
as though some spirit of the mountain had got inside her and
was using her, making a burning bush of her, to hide a voice.

Sonja, looking at the circle of faces, felt as though their
mouths, which were still safely engaged in eating, had fallen
open. The circle seemed to gape and stare at Liv, and there was
that smile again marching across Astrid's expression like water
over-running a cup. Having something to do was no preservation. She had had something to do — nobody could have
studied more earnestly.... She ought never to have given up
her music. When she thought of Olaf always she regretted that

she had stopped playing. Stopped with the suddenness of a tree coming down in a storm. It was one of the things that was too late now, in the same category as having a daughter.

'Cooking! Cooking!' repeated Anna helplessly, and wished that Astrid would stop grinning.

'If I must take up something, I may as well take up something that will be useful.'

'Quite right,' agreed her Uncle Johan. He thought it was a splendid idea. There could not be very much the matter with a girl who wanted to learn to cook. 'You let her go,' he said to Anna, 'and don't wear your nerves out fretting about her. She'll be all right, as right as rain; she'll be like Sonja, she'll have enough of it.... She'll never want to go away again!'

This time Sonja, blind to the circle, felt the gape within her. A thrust that split her open, letting the blood run out of the belief and courage and the beauty of the day, sending her spirit, pale and staggering amidst its own shadows, where nobody went but she, where nobody knew. Liv seemed to be knocking there, knocking and crying: 'Open! It is time! It is time!' And Time itself came to an end. She waited, pressing against walls that were giving way upon her, for Anna's voice. It came ... leaving the walls still standing:

'If it has the same effect upon her as it had upon Sonja it will be all right.'

Yes, yes. It would be all right. Liv was different. She belonged to a harder age, more trustworthy. Liv was too proud (see how she had retrieved herself and them, wiping the humiliation out of her flight in that fine sweep of the truth), too courageous, too ... sentient, and aware, for shipwreck. There could scarcely be two fools in the same family, such as the fool that she herself had been. Johan was right, right in his muscular male way — it was wrong to make a fuss about it, quite wrong and silly. She was relieved when Anna said, as though their minds had arrived simultaneously at the terminus:

'Well, I suppose it is best to let you go!'

It fell on Liv like rain, blessed rain on the parched suspense of her patience. There! It was done. And like rain, it washed the dryness out of her. Impulsively she brushed Olaf away and, leaning across him, kissed her mother on the cheek. 'Mother...' she broke out and did not end it. The word was like a seed, sown in the moment between them, making fertile that which had been fallow, so that years afterwards they were to remember, sheltering under the tree's branches, the quick spring of their sympathy.

Olaf pushed back into his place again, separating them. 'I wish you wouldn't go,' he protested.

'When you are a big boy you'll go, too!' she answered.

'No! Never, never! I'll stay here...' he gave the promise to Sonja, 'as long as you stay!'

'That's right,' Sonja said gently, as though the mere acceptance would break it. It was a boy's promise, meant, like all the vows of youth, for a man's breaking. But it made her feel very grand, and full of homage to take it. The time was ripe now for her to point to the dicky bird on the ceiling, so she said to Johan, giving him the steadiest eyes of indifference: 'Do you think we could get round by Sulitelma? Anna would like to see the mines, and home in time...' she carried the smile that she had been holding back ever since his vow of fidelity, to Olaf, 'in time for Olaf to go to bed!' She knew that she was disappointing him, letting him down over a small thing when he had been so splendid about a great one, and she added instantly, before the disappointment spread through him, 'not really for you to go to bed, darling, you can have another late night, but we must absolutely get back at your bed hour, so that you can have your supper before it is too late.' If he did not have it punctually, and was allowed to stay up, then he would be sure to have nightmares about Hulder flying at him with her tail up and all her wiles flying.

Liv was convinced that she owed her mother's consent to Aunt Sonja, but she did not dare to look at her or show by the slightest sign of recognition that she believed so; for her mother, she was aware, would be sure to construe it into an alliance. She was specially nice to her mother, staying behind her when, after lunch, in the climb to the snow-cap, she failed to keep up with the others. Anna accepted her manner at her own value — cupboard love, she called it to herself. 'It's only because I'm letting her go. Mind you,' she still felt cross about it, 'I expect you to learn to cook, cook Norwegian dishes as well as French ... and I expect you to come back and marry Harald and settle down in Mornesund.'

Liv said: 'I'll do my best.' She would certainly learn to cook, it would always come in useful, but Harald ... Harald, she hoped, would find somebody else, and she thought of Astrid, and imagined her at Mornesund, in the lovely Mornesund garden, with the yellow violets and the Hardanger roses, and where, looking from the windows of what had been Fru Christensen's bedroom, you could see the silver streaks of the Hyttefoss.

Going home, with the car crawling downwards like a burrowing animal, Sonja did not once allow herself to catch

Liv's eyes. She was assisted by Liv, who was playing the same
game. There were times when the road was so steep and
perilous that they seemed suspended between the heights
behind and the depths below. The Rindalsholm yawned to
receive them. As they caught on to the edge of the forest they
could smell the sharp, pungent odour of the tar being tapped
from the trees. The pines shone as they passed, heedless of
their bleeding, the trunks passed swiftly, changing with the
shadows, changing places with each other, like people running to see the king pass by ... the king and his merry men.
Sonja's being belonged here, and bloomed with the kinship.
She was sister to every sign they passed, the blue-grey rocks,
the firs, the mountain grasses, the whitened crevices where
water rushed and snow lay and sun said: 'Be born again, for
heaven is close and God so near that only blindness keeps
him hidden.' In these high wastes she had resolved much.
She had come back from that far journey — which Liv was
about to take — to discover in this place the meaning of her
race and of her own soul. Her sons had been born of that
meaning. From beginning to end the Viking would last in
them, the going forth and the return, the return to the snows,
the everlasting snows, and though the mother in her cried
out against it, she knew that they would go out into the
world's scatter and spend and waste this secret, but the secret
would remain greater than all their scattering. It would be
conscience to them and redemption. It would, when the
waste was done, fold their hands and send them down into
the earth as the old kings had gone down into their ships.
Yielding to these thoughts as the car sped home her belief in
Liv quickened. The girl had that spirit, the spirit of her race.

The ice of her youth might thaw in her, break her like any torrent over a foss, but the snows would whiten out again ... the snows would save her....

No, she was no longer afraid. It had happened now, and the girl was going. There would be no need for her to run away. She would go with the trumpets of encouragement blowing about her, and all their thoughts standing up to her like soldiers. She would have to return the salute, to remember, down there, to return it, not to forget it.

When they got to Sulitelma, Anna was too tired to get out of the car and go with the others to inspect the pits. Sonja did not want to go because she hated the mines. She kept it hidden from Johan, listening with an excessive indulgence to cover up her dislike whenever he discussed them with her. She and Anna stayed together in the car. She was glad, because it meant that they would say what had to be said about Liv, and afterwards she would be free to talk to the girl herself. She began directly, as soon as the others were out of hearing: 'I'm glad, Anna, you're letting her go!'

Anna interrupted her sharply: 'I simply do not understand you! Do you want her to be ruined? Did it make you so happy that you want somebody else to fall into it?'

She was silent, taking the stab and extracting it before she spoke. 'If I thought, Anna, that she was going to go through what I went through, I'd give my life to prevent her!' Her voice was passionate, as though her instincts forced her to convince her sister, and passion was the only way. Anna was truly sore about it. 'Oh, don't you see,' she cried, genuinely sorry for her, 'that the child was eating her heart to go, that she'd made up her mind, that it was holding her back from this boy, Harald Christensen?'

'You think that, Sonja; you really and truly believe that?'

'Yes,' she said, 'I do.'

'I'll give her six months.'

Sonja said nothing. She thought: if you can get her back in six months then she'll have found out, sooner than I did. 'I wasn't in league with her,' she explained, not to defend herself, but to exonerate Liv. 'It was quite by accident that we began to talk about it. I told her that she must never, never for a moment let herself forget that she is betrothed to Harald Christensen.'

'You did, oh, you did? Oh, I am glad! That's a good thing. No, she must never forget it. The boy is crazy about her.'

'I didn't mean, of course, that she would let him down, Anna.' No. It wasn't to save the boy, but to save the girl herself that she had said it, so that she should not let herself down. She was far more likely to do that than to betray anybody. She was the sort that kept herself shut like a tabernacle....

Johan came back with Liv. 'Erik has taken Astrid to watch the copper silted.'

'Mud!' Liv cried. 'Mud, and little glints! I saw it all.'

'Liv,' Johan continued, 'refused to go.' He laughed at her, delighting to see the confusion running through her. 'She hated it, like as I hate it. He loves her,' Sonja reasoned, 'because she is young, because he sees me in her and can forget me.'

She was silent as they drove, after that, along the edge of the forest. The forest grew on the mountain like tufts of hair; the trees, so grand in themselves, meant nothing at all to the mountain, no more that the hair on his face meant to a man. Stortoppen was aloof. Mountain and fjord, they were the twin terms of her country, the twin signs of the spit of primal lava that had shot up rocks for the first footholds of mankind. 'And when Earth dies,' she thought, 'it will be from these heights that humanity will take the last leap into the fathomless air of eternity. We have,' she smiled to herself, 'done all that could possibly be done with water, from streams to glaciers, from pools to fjords, from trickles over stones to cataracts.' Nothing lured men into adventure like vast tracts of water, unless — now that they had begun to traverse it — the vast tracts of the sky ... another sea. The earth lay at the bottom of the sky, all its objects waving, as sea-weed, and the marine forests lay at the bottom of the ocean.

On the steps of her home she lingered, letting Anna go in, and Astrid. Liv waited too. The sun was so close upon the valley, a great golden entrance through which heat burned. One had only, it seemed, to go forward a pace or two and find the heat blaze upon one's cheek. Liv and she stood together, a strange unity between them. Even without speech, Sonja felt, the understanding was there. It made her slow to speak. 'You will go now, you will go to Paris!'

'Yes,' said Liv, 'I shall go.'

They were silent, infused with the sunny light, watching the valley where the red and white houses shone like flowers. 'Do you not feel,' Sonja asked in a voice full of dreams, 'that it is a great thing to have been born here?'

There came back to Liv the mood of love in which she had said good-bye to Odda, the rapture that had linked her to the Seven Sisters, the pain of a worship that she had not understood until now. 'Yes,' she said simply.

'And you are going away from it!'

Suddenly she was rooted, caught, in the soil of her people. It was odd how, without meaning to (for she was certain that her aunt did not mean deliberately to entrap her), the wildness went out of her, the roving spirit that had filled her with thirst and hunger became appeasable and limitable. Beyond it, and in the very midst of its satisfactions, there would always be this — this moment with Aunt Sonja, this … initiation, this knowing where one belonged and the mould of one's fashioning. She seemed to grow up in an instant into a deep knowledge of her direction. She said: 'I shall come back.'

'Of course, you will come back!' She wanted to ask, 'But what will bring you back?' It depended upon that. There were some who drifted hither and thither, uncaring, seeing in every land the mirage of their hopes. There were some who were sent back, as she had been, to pay for the faith that she had broken. She had built it up again, in her sons, in the love she had given Johan, in her own solitudes.

'You know, Liv,' she said gently, 'we are very emancipated, we Norwegian women; there's a free spirit in us. It is not only that we are, in this age, if you like, the daughters of Ibsen' (she saw a young woman rapping on the Master Builder's table) 'but it goes farther. We are the daughters of the Vikings.'

'Daughters of the Vikings' went ringing through Liv's head. Sons and daughters of the Vikings, and her race went marching — a million Birkebeins — through the snows of centuries.

'It is very real to me here,' Sonja continued, 'but…' she made a gesture towards beyond the sunset, 'down there it seemed not to matter, to be very long ago, dead … it is not dead. It is in us, and will remain with us until we perish. It ought … perhaps it does (she did not want to preach) save us from peril. When we are young, you know, Liv, we think that we can do anything, especially with ourselves. Isn't that so?'

She was pleading (trying to hide it), pleading with her own ghost in Liv's body, the youth that would never come back to her. 'Down there, Liv, there is so much that is beautiful, a marvel, all made with hands, they have done such wonderful things — human beings, they have learned how to do it, had the energy, that sort of energy.' And suddenly she could not go on. It seemed so stupid to say to a young girl like Liv (Liv was not stupid) that in Norway the energy had been taken from them rather than given to them by nature, they had been made to serve. The mountains had drawn them, drawn the entrails out of their souls, emptied them, let the dreams blow through. She felt that. She felt it so intensely that she had come to regard the dreams, all that music that flew through one, as the chief thing in life. It mattered because it wiped away profanity. It held one's head against an immense bosom, where one could feel the heart beating and never see the hands or feet or face.

'It must be wonderful…' Liv answered, 'the rest of the world.'

'Very wonderful,' she agreed, and felt her wits in prison. Nothing could go out that was not the merest surface of what one felt. She tried to rescue the purpose with which she had begun: 'Do not ever,' she admonished, 'be afraid of the snow. They boast…' again she made that sweep of her hand, 'of the sun. Look!' she cried out, 'have we not the sun here, so close that we can look into his eyes?' She saw Liv's hands tighten, and reward flared through her. 'Come!' there was an excited throb in her voice. 'Come, we must not kept them waiting!' She slipped her arm through the girl's and drew her into the house.

* * * *

Liv's thoughtfulness towards her mother remained. It was not pure cupboard love, after all, Anna realised, and was in turn kinder to her elder daughter. Having granted the girl's wish, and its inevitability, there remained nothing to quarrel about. And also, seeing that none of them, with the exception of spells of schooling at Oslo, had ever been separated before, there grew into the weeks immediately before Liv's departure, a forbearance with each other that was quite ominous to Liv, although she offered it herself, as well as being the main participant. Astrid made her a new dress and helped her with her sewing, and all of them spoke French. Her Aunt Sonja never spoke to her again with the intimacy of the day on which they had gone to Stortoppen. She became aloof again, going ways that were completely her own in her home. These were days when she was a complete stranger to Liv, glancing at her with a coldness that froze her. She was like a portrait more than a real woman, a portrait of somebody you remembered and wished they were alive again. Liv was driven from the repulse into the warmth of her mother's and Astrid's affection. Of them she was, at least, sure. They did not go up and down like a see-saw. They never took you up into a great height and dropped you down, sent you spinning until you landed. Aunt Sonja would come into a room when she was there and take no notice of her. She would, perhaps, go over to her bureau and begin to write a letter, and sit there, pausing between the lines, making it up before your eyes, and never say a word. Or she would look at her down the length of the dinner-table and ask her if she wanted a second helping: 'And you, Liv? Do you want some more of this,' or that, or whatever it was. She would answer: 'No, thank you, Aunt Sonja,' and the business of it was ended. Never a smile, never a touch of remembrance, as of one who said: 'We know, don't we?' No. The communion was completely broken. It was like something that had been painted into her, framed (by the day on the mountain) and done with. The only time that Sonja was not hidden was with her son Olaf. She could not hide then, for, having once revealed herself, Liv beheld in everything that she gave the boy the woman who was escaping her. She was hurt. It was as though she denied Liv any morsel of that woman.

It was not that Sonja deliberately shut herself against the girl's devotion, but she reacted with terrible pride from the revelation on the mountain. She had peeled there, before Liv's eyes, the protecting skin off her soul, and now the skin had swiftly grown back again. Nothing was to be gained by repeating the operation. She had recovered control and life went on with its habitual smoothness, in which the visit of her sister and her nieces was a mere ingredient. Liv owed her nothing ... not yet, so she could not bear to take all that the girl with the generosity and impulsiveness of her youth was prepared to offer. It would have been like thieving the years ahead from her — from both of them. And she, who so well knew the value of those 'years ahead' could not endure any mortgage of them. And also she was forced to withdraw herself, for every item of Liv's departure evoked bitter memories of her own. She saw in Liv the girl she had been, and was filled with an immense hatred of the waste she had made of it. It would be different with Liv. She was a younger and maturer generation ... (if any younger generation can ever be that), and it did not by any means follow that because she had made a poor fool of herself that another girl should. She reasoned it in every way, but, over and beyond all the powers of reason, she came gradually to see herself in Liv and to resent the resemblance. All that she had suppressed since her marriage arose and tore her to pieces every time she thought of the girl. This attitude frightened her with its tyranny. In order to avoid it she avoided Liv. That was the secret. It was as though she said, from her secret depths to the secret depths in Liv: do wrong and I shall despise you, as though any wrongdoing of Liv's would be a repetition of her own. And then, suddenly, she would love the girl so passionately that she wanted to prevent her from going away, going out of the country. Once, when she and Liv accidentally stooped to caress Olaf together, she felt like taking them both in her arms, like saying: 'Stay here, and I shall shelter you.' She had been strong enough not to do it.

She went her own ways in her own house, forgetting nothing, hiding what she felt. And, of course, it was only right that she should leave the girl to Anna. She was Anna's girl....

It was first of all decided that Liv should go practically immediately in order to go with Barbra Grondahl, who was going from Oslo to Hamburg, early in August. Fru Evensen never liked the idea. It was Johan who persuaded her to accept it. She had said: 'I do not like that girl, and I hope that you will not see very much of her.' She made Johan impatient. It was at breakfast-time and he turned upon her with his mouth full of flatbröd. 'What's wrong with the girl?'

Sonja saw the conviction stutter in Anna's mouth as she kept it back. He repeated the question (he hated women who became flustered irrationally): 'What's she done?'

'She's done nothing, of course.' Nothing that would stand up to her brother-in-law's acceptance and repel it. When Barbra was a little girl she had a habit of putting ordures into those tiny satin-lined boxes, in which jewellers pack rings and brooches, and, tying them up with string, she would drop them out of the window and watch how people behaved when they found and opened them in the street below. It caused her endless and incredible amusement to do this. And it seemed to Anna Evensen that a girl — a girl of quite good family — who could do that was no fit companion for the daughters of the Odda pastor. 'I don't like her,' she said honestly, and with such soundness in her voice that Johan believed her.

'You may have cause, and you may be mistaken, but I think that Liv ought to go with somebody who has already been.' He added, twinkling at her as he buttered more flatbröd, 'Better the devil you know than the devil you don't know.'

'But Liv needn't consort with devils.'

'She might entertain them, like the angels, unawares.'

'Exactly, but all the same!' She shook her head.

'She's very amusing,' Astrid told him. 'She's an artist. She paints red foxes.'

'She paints red foxes.'

The bright little red foxes seemed to run over the tablecloth.

And Liv said, helping Astrid and defending the absent Barbra: 'She's not so wild as she used to be.'

'How can you tell?' her mother demanded, and everybody looked at Liv — to watch, it seemed, the psychology of her friend's change work in her.

She glanced at her Aunt Sonja and instantly away from her, and said simply: 'She tells you about it now ... she never used to.'

Sonja thought: 'It has run out of her into the little red foxes.'

In the end Liv did not go with Barbra Grondahl. It made her departure too hurried, and Anna, in spite of her acceptance of the arrangement outwardly, never liked it. Liv, on her side, did not want to go to Oslo, for it would have meant, she knew, a scene with Harald, who would have come up from Hardanger to see her off. It was decided that, before her mother and Astrid returned to Odda, she should go to Bodo and from there direct to France. A room was booked for her in a little hotel in Paris where Sonja had stayed years ago. It was Sonja who gave the address to Anna. 'It may not be there now,' she said, 'but if it is, it will be all right, I think. It was charming, years ago, when I stayed there. I had a room overlooking a tiny courtyard with a garden full of marigolds and mignonette.'

She and Anna and Liv and Astrid were sitting by the big open windows of the drawing-room, and Anna had looked up and said: 'Would it not be better if you wrote?'

'No, no!' she answered, and made a fault in her stitching.

Liv, with that vigilance that marked her manner towards her aunt, saw and wondered. What lay behind, so that after all these years it could make her make a fault in her stitching? She said, coldly (for Aunt Sonja was frozen very far away from her that day): 'Weren't you happy there, Aunt Sonja?' The impertinence instantly scalded through her. But she did not show that she regretted it. She evaded her aunt's eyes. She looked straight in front of her, out of the window, as if the answer was of no consequence, and she did not expect to be answered. But, just as clearly as though she was actually looking at her, she saw her aunt's head go up from the broken stitch, and was aware of the hidden trouble in her eyes; she felt it leaping and quivering like a live thing under the cheerfulness of her aunt's voice:

'Very, Liv ... extremely happy.'

'How covert they were,' she said to herself, rethreading her needle, full of the stupidest, the cruellest curiosities. It was always there, if you scratched deep enough — the desire to throw Christians to the lions. There was an emperor of China whose special ecstasy arose from watching the extraction of teeth from quite innocent people, who wondered why it should be done to them. She felt a little of that innocence, answering Liv in whom the Emperor of China seemed to be manifesting himself. It occurred to her that she owed it to Anna to check-mate the Emperor, so she added: 'Liv ought to be all right there, it's in the open part at the end of Boulevard Raspail. In any case, as it is the only address I can think of and you do not wish her to stay with this Grondahl girl, you might send her there until she is able to hunt out a place for herself.'

The Emperor of China expired.

A few minutes later Sonja put down her sewing and went out into the garden. Liv wanted to go out after her, to say that she was sorry. But she knew that it would be quite useless to do that. It was (when she tried to think why she had done it) just a random urge to make her aunt feel, to prick her so that she might bleed a little. She was really sorry that she had done it. Her remorse stirred her to the other extreme. She felt that, once more, she had got inside her aunt and was at once happy about her, solaced by this slight prick of intimacy.

On the day of her going (her mother and Astrid and Erik were going with her to Bodo), Aunt Sonja came into her room. She shut the door and stood, looking particularly stately and queen-like, against it, without coming forward.

'Liv, will you write to me?'

She rose from her knees, and stood where she had risen. She was trembling inside like a tree that had been caught by the wind, but she did not show it: 'Yes, Aunt Sonja, I will write to you.'

Sonja looked at her. The light was behind her. She looked so slender, so young, so frail standing there, swaying imperceptibly, against the flood of sunshine. 'Not stiff little notes,' she said, 'not stiff little notes of politeness telling me about places that I know all about....'

Liv waited.

'Do you understand, Liv, I do not want you to write to me just because you must send a letter ... in case I should forget you. I shall not forget. I only want you to write to me when...' it was difficult to find words for her meaning without forecasting some doom. 'Well, Liv, if there is nobody else.' A slow smile rose up into Liv's face. It embarrassed her.

It made her add: 'I don't mean that everybody else in the world will be wiped out, but ... oh, you'll see,' she said it quite gaily, 'I may seem the only one ... at the moment.' She set its circumference by that 'moment'.

Liv was stroking her dress with her hands. She gathered a piece of her skirt into her fingers and said: 'Yes, I will write.'

'Thank you. I shall write to you.' She meant that she would write back at once, but it would have been foolish to say it. 'I am not a great letter-writer ... as you know.' Her letters to the Odda household had been few and far between.

'I know,' Liv smiled, 'they were as scarce as birthdays.'

They stood looking at each other and each remembering their first greeting. It seemed to Liv that a slice out of her life had been extracted during the weeks that she had passed in her aunt's house. She was not the same girl who had first come there. She was no longer the child that she had been.

Sonja felt very old looking at her, old and dried, a tree in which the sap could not mount for many more years. She was wrung with misery, and was saved by her intelligence, by a splendid sense of the futility of words. 'I shall think of you often, dear child,' she said, and went and kissed her. 'I am glad that you came.'

'I wish...' Liv's voice was meditative, withheld, 'that I was not going so soon.'

'But your mother is going directly afterwards. You would not have waited! You know, you are getting what you wished for!' Like all wishes come true the salt had gone out of it. She would recover. The taste would come back. It was quite natural that she should feel as she was feeling.

'I know.' Liv made a wry face. She wondered if this was her aunt's good-bye. It seemed so inadequate, such a mockery. Her aunt was there and she was not there, like a fern enclosed in a block of ice. The contact was absent.

Sonja straightened the eiderdown on the bed. She knew that she was failing the girl, but it was only on the surface, only on the surface. The child did not realise that there was no need to cram everything into the first five minutes. There were days to come, years to come. Youth could never wait, and everything came, Life taught you how to wait. You went round and round the little circle and ended where you began, round and round, summer after summer, and winter after winter — the darkened, sunless winters that she loved now because of their strange sense of pregnancy. The days lay in them as in a womb, folded and full of growth, and during them she used to hold her home (as Time held the world) locked into her love, locked and warmed and guarded in that substance which is the breath of life. Without it no sun can blow heat in you. 'I will go now,' she said, looking at Liv with these thoughts in her head.

Some impulse moved Liv to cross the room and open the door for her, show her out as though she were a visitor. There was a smile on Sonja's face as she went through the doorway. Perhaps she was thinking that — about being a visitor in her own house. Liv flushed and was cross because she had done it.

They said good-bye again, casually, before the others, on the steps. Uncle Johan gave her a great hug and tucked her into the car. 'Be a good girl and come back to your mother and settle down and marry!'

'Yes, yes!' she laughed, 'I shall do all those things.' She was trying to clutch her will into a resolve not to look at her aunt at the last minute, to let the car turn and wheel and pass and leave her standing there. But, of course she looked, and their eyes met. Her aunt never moved, she looked rigid, like a wooden soldier glued to a disc. Liv's hand shot out and waved to her. She cried out to her from the remotest corners of her mind and heart: 'Wave to me, Aunt Sonja! Wave to me!' But Aunt Sonja did not wave. The car had almost wheeled completely round the clump of German firs, speeding to the very last moment; when they could no longer see each other, then (as though the little wooden soldier had been struck by lightning) Aunt Sonja moved. She did not wave, but her arms shot out as they had shot out to her that first sunny night upon the step, and it was Liv who was rigid, who appeared rigid, for her aunt vanished, and there was only the clump of German firs and Liv's hand clenched under the rug which Uncle Johan had tucked round her. She suffered one of those moments which are so horrible when one is young, those moments of frustration when the warmth of life shrivels to an ash, when we are burned to the core and done with. Trangfoss and the car hummed together, and through blinding tears, which stayed in her eyes without falling, she saw the mountains in mists of beauty dancing beyond, and the valley, into which they were descending, seemed filled with a pearly liquid morning. The tears ran into her throat, and she saw the seams of Erik's coat making *fleur-de-lys* lines on his back in front of her, and her mother was lamenting a thermos flask that had, or had not, been forgotten.

Chapter Three

She entered Paris on a September afternoon, emerging in a taxi from the usual grey drab of the station — of all stations — into a glow of sunshine, into hot, whitened strips of asphalt upon which people and their shadows swarmed with amazing energy. Strong, dark people, men with bodies rammed into the tightest clothes, and deep-bosomed, dark-eyed women, from whom voices rose and floated with an emphasis that struck harshly against her ears, like the tuning up of instruments in an orchestra that was directly about to perform some splendid work. It would be wonderful when one knew what it was all about. She was excited by the glow, the colour and the movement, by the swift sweep of her taxi through old streets that rose and flashed out of old engravings seen amongst her father's books. She recognised the Place de la Concorde before she saw the name, saying to herself: 'This must be the Place de la Concorde,' and thought of that other Concord where Thoreau was able so magnificently to despise the need for letters, before she saw, beyond the hard space where the traffic skated, beyond the fleece-filled needles of the fountains, kneeling in the blaze of the September sunshine, kneeling eternally amongst the crowds that were Paris, poor Marie Antoinette without her head, which had fallen and was dripping by the little spaniel, who licked the drip, drip, as though he could preserve by this act of love the flow from which his dear mistress had already died. Poor little spaniel, poor queen, poor thrones and kingdoms. It helped to serve the justice for which the people were crying out, confusing it (just because they were hungry) with bread and pearl necklaces.

There was the river, the flowing Seine, shining green and with an unexpected clearness, funny little men dangling toy fishing rods into it for what, she felt certain, remembering her native salmon, could only be minnows. The tricolour drooped, wilted like a flower in the bright sunshine, out of an official, stern-walled building, and the taxi ran through little crooked streets, like wrinkles on an aged face, in and out, full of varying expressions, then up through a boulevard which she saw, by and by, was Raspail, at the end of which (as Aunt Sonja had told her) was her hotel.

She stood in the entrance hall amidst her trunks and peered into the dark well of the bureau which descended by steps from the street level, and rang the bell. She saw an opposite door open, and a blonde lady sailed and expanded into the bureau like one of those Japanese flowers which opens and enlarges itself in water before your eyes. Liv introduced herself in the French which she had never spoken out of her own country. The lady immediately grasped who she was and accepted her with an extraordinary seriousness, with the air of one completely withdrawn, torn momentarily from some world of her own beyond the door which she had opened, and where Liv and the attention she demanded had no place. But she looked from Liv to the room beyond the bureau and shouted from deep lungs: 'It is the Norwegian lady. She is to have *la chambre de la comtesse*, isn't she?' and at the same time she took a key from a board, and with the key in her hand and the assent from the hidden room buzzing in her ears, she led Liv through the hall across a courtyard and up two flights of stairs to *la chambre de la comtesse*. Somebody whose name was Julienne was to bring up her luggage. Liv thanked her, breathed fervently a prayer with what air was left from her gasp up the stairs that she would go, go, go quickly. She wanted her to go before she could see what she was thinking. She went, and closed the door, and Liv turned, dazed, as though the taxi had dashed with her into a wall. It was the most squalid room that she had ever seen. The paper was bulging in great blisters from the walls. The mirror above the stove was blurred, the mercury had melted and was running in streams through the blur as rivers run through a map. It resembled a map more than a mirror. The bed was humped and untidy, the floor carpetless and not as clean as one expected a carpetless floor to be. She was baffled by every effort of her imagination to believe that her aunt had been here. She went to the window and looked out, hoping at least to find the flower-beds. But no flower-beds were there. Long ago, a child, she had read in her first French story-book, of a gendarme who was very cross with a lady who had her windows filled with boxes of mignonette. They had taken the window-boxes away. They were a menace to the people who walked underneath them, so they had been taken away. There were no flowers. This was Paris and there were no flowers in the garden. And then, that other book in which Napoleon upset the old woman's apple-cart in Ajaccio.

He had upset a lot of apple-carts, gone on as he had begun. She saw the retreat from Moscow running over like an apple out of a cart, and Napoleon running away and hiding from the old woman. They had burnt Moscow, as Cortes had burnt his boats. It was called cutting off your nose to spite your enemy's face. Julienne rapped at the door and came in. She was dark, and her face, framed in the blue handkerchief which she had tied round her hair to preserve it from the dust, was the face of the girl in the corner of a five-franc note. She had the face of France, aged a little, for she was about thirty-five years of age, a thirty-five-years-old France, beautiful and mellow and brooding over tilled fields and vineyards. 'Bonjour, madame!'

Yes, she is France, and I am not a madame, Liv thought and smiled at her. 'What sort of a hotel is this?' she asked.

Julienne shrugged shoulders. 'What can you expect?' she demanded. 'It has changed owners so often, and now...' she seemed to scratch flies out of space, 'packed with Russians.'

'Russians!' Revolutions, and steppes, and Lenins.

'Yes, Russians. Listen! Upstairs above you, there is an old general, oh, a celebrated general; he owned a lot of *terre* (the word remained *terre* in Liv's mind) and now ... what do you think, imagine! He sells postcards in the street, and his daughter works in a factory!'

'And the *comtesse*?' Liv asked. 'The *comtesse* who was here!' It could not be true, she had been thinking, but with the general above it became feasible.

'She was so pretty, *divorcée*, a Hungarian, she left....'

'Yes, why did she leave?' Liv felt that she had to find out for it might give her a clue to her own departure.

Julienne had begun to rake out the stove. 'Oh, that's a story! I'll tell you, but...' she nodded in the direction of the courtyard which led to the bureau, 'never say a word. She met a young man, a beautiful young man, in a restaurant, and he had no money and nowhere to sleep, so she paid for his dinner and she brought him home, and ... shared her bed with him. Oh, she was most generous! She had an open heart, and, there you are! He stole away in the middle of the night, at daybreak, and took her purse with him. All her money. She had no money to pay. She wept, but the *patron*! Oh, you know, the *patron* he is hard as a stone....'

Well, Liv thought, swept into spaces she had never dreamed of, she would not have to leave for that reason. It was quite clear that it was not the same hotel that it had been when Aunt Sonja had stayed here. She would stay for this one night, and in the morning, when she was not so tired, when she would be less excited, she would go out and find some place that was not ... packed with Russians. She was hungry, hungry and tired. She asked Julienne if there was a dining-room where she could have something to eat, and was told that they did not provide food in the hotel. She pointed at the stove: 'The *locataires* did for themselves!' It was a 'funny hotel', she said to herself, and turned down the coverlet to examine the bed. There were no sheets on it. That meant that they would be clean sheets. Clean sheets. And no flowers in the garden. She must send a card to say that she had arrived, that she had found the hotel, but that she was leaving because there were no flowers in the garden. No. It would be better not to write until tomorrow until she had found something else, then she would be able to give them her address. Julienne returned with her box, aided by somebody who remained in the corridor. She found some francs for the one who remained in the corridor and gave it to Julienne, who passed it out to — it might have been a man or a woman. She asked for a towel, and had to wait while Julienne disappeared again. The cinders from the stove were lying on the floor on a piece of newspaper with square letters, Hungarian probably, left by the countess, the countess who had a good heart. The young man had taken all she had. Give all thou hast. There was a boy blowing a trumpet on the lace panel on the window, a fat, naked boy, meant for a three-year-old cherub. A boy blowing a tin trumpet in a courtyard where there were no flowers. Outside the window a beautiful deep voice called like music, like a dove in a wood: 'Katusha! Katusha!' and again 'Katusha! Katusha!' and across snows, snows vaster than the snows between her own fjords, she heard that voice calling in loneliness and sorrow: Sonia from Dostoevsky, Anna from Tolstoy, all the women from Moscow to Siberia, from Siberia to Ekaterinburg, and there was Julienne with the towel. 'Thank you,' she said, and returned from Russia to France, and darted straightaway to the moment when Aunt Sonja had made a fault in her stitching and gone away to hide it, gone into the deep blue flowers that dropped down like udders from the tree in the Rindalsholm garden. This was the hotel in which Aunt Sonja had stayed. The same and not the same ... like 'the king is dead, long live the king!' The old hotel was dead. There was another voice in the courtyard.

Julienne peeped through the lace cherub. 'Oh, the poor general!' she exclaimed. 'The *pauvre homme*! His daughter, you know, sleeps in the bed and he sleeps on the floor!'

Liv's thoughts commented on Julienne's chatter: 'Bivouac! Bivouac!' She found a clean handkerchief and pair of gloves and went out to dine.

She spent the evening writing letters to her mother and Astrid, and notes to Harald and Olaf, saying in each of them that she would not post them until she could send them her new address. She sent her love to Aunt Sonja. Nothing more, yet it was to Aunt Sonja more than to any of them that she truly wanted to write. She wanted to tell Aunt Sonja everything — about the general who slept on the floor, about the poor little countess, about the Russian voices, everything, and she told her nothing; and to the others she wrote careful and guarded letters, mentioning everything with a film over it, so that it should only be seen through veils darkly and would not alarm them. She went to bed and read *Kristin Lavransdatter* until she dropped off to sleep.

Hours afterwards she awoke in pitch blackness, roused and torn for an unknown reason from the land of lost consciousness into a state in which it took her several seconds to recover it. She came back from the light before the darkness, from *Kristin Lavransdatter*, who was digging in a field to find the letter that she had written to her mother, digging with tremendous hacks into the hard earth to find the letter which she had written to her mother, from all this to the tumult that was happening above her, the resounding thuds which had awakened her. She switched on the light. The bleak, bare bulb glittered high up on the ceiling, covered with fly-specks. The ceiling itself was covered with fly-specks. Some of them moved. She shut her eyes upon a world that had gone crazy under the glitter of the poor little fly-

blown star of light. Twinkle, twinkle, little star, oft I wonder
what you are! She did really wonder if the specks upon the
ceiling had moved. She opened her eyes wide and steadily,
and fixed them upon one black spot near the bulging
wallpaper and timed it, like a horse in a race, to reach the
wall. It moved. It moved at the rate of a mile a lifetime. Her
wits played Achilles to its tortoise, and both won. The spot
reached the wall and disappeared. She jumped out of the
bed. Up above her the Russian general was thumping on
the door of the bedroom, which his daughter had most
evidently shut against him. He battered and (although she
could not understand a word until, having recourse to
French, as though to an audience, he began to cry out to
her to open the door), she was aware from the tones of his
voice how he abused and pleaded in turn. At intervals she
heard him collapse in a heap on the floor, muttering like
old King Lear. Then once more the battering would begin.
She saw the shaggy, bearded old man ramming his fists
upon the dark door of night which shut him out into a
world where one sold postcards in the street. Lear had
travelled a few centuries to sell those postcards, and
Goneril, home from the factory, had her own reasons....
Long ago, a little child, he had fondled her and taken
delight in her, and now she had shut her door against him.
She had a son in an orphanage, her husband had run away
from her, Julienne had said. Everybody in this hotel seemed
to have run away from somebody or something.
Somewhere the heralds had blown their horns, blown them
against a horizon with a flaming sky and the burnt crests of
trees, and people had taken to flight.... She dressed as

quickly as possible, thinking that she would go up to the old man and say to him that he could have her room. If she clicked her heels together and saluted him, and addressed him as general, he might even go out and get a taxi for her and she could go right away to Barbra Grondahl's studio and wake her and say: Please let me sleep on the floor. I can't stay where I am. There are *punaises* on the ceiling, and a Russian general battering the door in the corridor. She looked at her watch: it was half-past three. She looked out of the window. No moon, and the courtyard a well of darkness. It would be madness to stumble through that darkness with Lear and her luggage — he with her trunk and she with the two valises! They would fall over each other. She went over to Goneril's side and decided to keep her door shut, and wait for dawn. She sat down under the light to read *Kristin Lavransdatter*, and was so tormented by the fear of what might drop on her head that she opened her umbrella and held it over her, thinking — this is much worse than rain....

Day broke gently against the lace cherub, a fume of smoke like fire lighted, and then silver, and then the lovely flush of the east and clouds running to the melting. She opened her window to watch it gather against the battlements of undefined buildings, urging the night to go and let the day come in; and ships went sailing out against the wind, and banners flew, and fish turned in the waters, and the voice of birds and mankind rose out of the darkness. Every lizard-point of the earth showed against the dawn. She thought of Eidenkollen, washed by the Sorfjorden, a snow of gulls upon it. And up above her she heard the snores of the Russian general....

Barbra opened the door after she had rung six times. Her long eyes were filled with sleep: 'Liv! Liv ... Evensen!'

'I had to come! I'd have knocked till Doomsday! Forgive me? You will, when you hear all about it, go back....' She pushed Barbra into the safety of the room, while she dealt with the taxi and her luggage. 'Oh, Barbra!' she cried, shutting the door, 'this is an invasion, but you said I was to come whenever I wanted to. I had to come. I don't know where I should have been without you, without your being here.'

'It's all right, Liv. You're most welcome, my dear young thing, as long as you don't object to company!' She pointed beyond Liv, who was still standing at the entrance to the studio, to the divan from which she had apparently risen. Sitting up in it was a tousled and smiling young man, who said, with a cheekiness that had to be pardoned by the hour, and the situation:

'Good morning, mademoiselle. You have come very early!'

'Good morning!' She looked at Barbra, the woe straining through her was caught and rippled by the night she had had, sitting so absurdly under the electric light with an umbrella reading *Kristin Lavransdatter*, the Achilles and tortoise moment, by King Lear, by the cherub on the window-pane blowing that absurd trumpet, by her efforts to escape — nobody believing that she had paid for her room, and in the end she had been forced to enter the bureau and watch the blonde lady being awakened by the side of the *patron* — each of them with a head drooping over a side of the bed, and the lady's knees moving with a sudden spring under the pale face of the pierrot who gathered the counterpane into a peak in the middle. It was too much for her. She put her hands up to her face and shook with peals of laughter.

'Well,' said Barbra resentfully, 'it need not make you hysterical.'

'It isn't this ... only, it's everything!' She gulped, and went on shaking.

'Oh, you'll get used to it!'

Get used to sitting up under an umbrella! She had come to Paris to play Robinson Crusoe. 'Barbra!' she gasped, 'I can't help it ... I ... I've been playing Robinson Crusoe all night!'

The young man went off, then, into loud guffaws of laughter that accompanied and exaggerated her own, and then Barbra, looking from one to the other, collapsed on a heap by the toes of the young man and joined them. They rocked it out. It united and bound them together. They emerged from it joined by mirth into the most wonderful acceptance of each other.

'I've been sitting up ... on a chair, under an umbrella....'

'But why?'

'*Punaises* ... and a Russian general.... Oh! I must try to tell you! It was an old hotel Aunt Sonja knew, she stayed there years ago and I was to stay there until I had time to find what I wanted.... I could not stay ... it was packed with Russians.'

'Be careful,' Barbra warned, and indicated the dark young man, 'he is a Russian!'

'I hope,' she turned to him, the mirth still alive in her, 'that you are clean!'

'Quite! Now!' he answered, twinkling back at her. 'I wasn't in Lemnos.... A vile place, like a vast tract of ground cinnamon, where we were fed on lentils. I know what it is!'

'It is terrible.'

'His name is Sasha Noudjevski.'

'It must have been awful, especially if you were young and not quite sure why it should happen…. I'm like that.' Her ears took in that his name was Sasha Noudjevski, and she smiled the recognition to Barbra. Their voices were all running against each other, hiding something like the light under the bushel, keeping it hidden so that it should not shine out and destroy them. 'The poor Russian general was locked out. He sleeps in the same room as his daughter, and she locked him out. It was just above me and it woke me up. He hammered on the door all night.'

Sasha Noudjevski looked at Barbra and Barbra looked at him and said 'Fornication and incest!'

And then it was as though the light came out from under the bushel, and Liv blazed: 'No, no! They are so poor that they can only afford one room. He sleeps on the floor, she works in a factory and is becoming paralysed. She has a boy of twelve in an orphanage. She never sees him!'

'How do you know?' Barbra tormented, and laughed.

But Sasha's dark eyes under his tousled black hair were nostalgic. When he spoke his voice was brutal. 'He's a fool if he doesn't! He'll probably live to be a hundred, they're as tough as boars, those old ones! What a farce…!'

The mirth had gone down in Liv. She was standing in the middle of the room looking at Barbra and Sasha, and far, far away, like a cow-bell on the mountain, she heard 'Katusha! Katusha!' The dream had gone out of it. Poverty was cold, it took the cloak off sorrow. She wished that she had not been so cowardly, not run away, that she had stayed at the hotel. It wasn't the poverty, the sordid meanness, it was the *punaises*.... 'Don't laugh!' she begged against their profanity, hurt by it, 'don't....'

'My dear,' Barbra appealed to her, 'don't be stupid!'

'I'm not....' She retaliated, and felt like a fool before them.

'What you need,' declared Sasha, 'is a cocktail!' and leaped out of bed. She saw the hair on his insteps as he thrust his feet into a pair of enormous slippers. He was tall, as tall as she was. He came towards her.

'Since half-past three this morning I have been longing for a cup of coffee!' she said, not so much to him as against him.

He glided away from her to Barbra, who was examining her complexion in a hand-mirror, and seized her, hand-mirror and all, and danced down the floor, with her chanting time to their steps with the words: 'the lady shall have coffee ... since half-past three in the morning ... half-past three in the morning!' Barbra joined in with him, contributing sweet thin notes like shells under the deep swell of his. In her yellow pyjamas she looked like a daffodil folded in the dark leaf of his arms, for his pyjamas were green. Barbra's head was pale gold; it drooped, her pale hands drooped, one holding the mirror. They danced back again and stopped before Liv.

'Look at her, in a dream world!' Barbra teased. 'A Norwegian dream world. Bah!' she cried. 'Liv, don't be like that. Come down, my child, come down off the ice-pole and see Life as it is!'

'Give her time,' pleaded Sasha and went to mix his cocktail.

'Give her coffee!' responded Barbra, and went to prepare it.

Liv sat down in a big chair before one of Barbra's *Per Gynt* scenes. She was not in the least astonished. She had known

Barbra for too long to be astonished. But she hated being treated ... as Astrid treated Olaf. It wasn't necessary. Barbra's manner put a little sign on her brow, like the signs on the doors of the Jews before pogrom, which set her apart, so that others could take up that air of superiority and differentiation. She resented it before Sasha, who was a stranger. And it limited Barbra in her eyes, narrowed her down to the boundaries of a map on which were marked only the places that Barbra knew. Barbra had always been conceited, so cocksure of herself. Astrid knew how to deal with her.

Sasha pressed her again to have a cocktail. 'No, thank you,' she said, smiling her sweetest, 'I've never tasted one in my life. I've read about them, of course, and do you not think that I'd better begin with them a little later on in the day?'

He agreed, but added: 'Every hour is a cocktail hour.'

'You know,' she said maliciously, piling up the atmosphere that Barbra had established, and feeling that she was looking as virginal as possible in her mourning clothes. 'I'm a priest's daughter!'

He whistled. 'Whew! They're the worst....'

'It depends upon whether you want to be, or not!'

'You don't want to?' He was gaily interested in her.

She said nothing. He was a fatuous young man, to whom it was best to say nothing. She was not his sort and never would be, no more than she would ever be Barbra's.

'What have you come to Paris for?' he asked.

She said simply: 'To learn cooking.' There now, she thought, 'I've done it. I am placed for ever. I have become a cook.' Her mind made a grand flourish of it, and she felt herself become a cross between the cook and the duchess in the English story-book, ready to fling frying-pans and sauce-pans at young men who asked questions.

'If your cooking,' he said, 'is as beautiful....'

Barbra interrupted him. 'Ah! It has already begun. Leave her alone, Sasha, leave her alone.'

'How can anybody leave her alone?' he demanded ruefully, 'she's so paintable ... and she is going to be a cook.'

Barbra said positively, 'That isn't true, it can't be. Why did you tell him a lie?'

'It is true.'

'Because of Harald Christensen?'

'Don't!' Liv was spiked on the highest point of defensive-ness. 'Harald Christensen has nothing at all to do with it. I had to have something to do. It was the condition. What could I do? I chose cooking.' It was the mere lever which had accomplished her right to go. She had chosen it at random. She had no special desire to learn to cook. Anybody, she thought, could cook if they put their mind to it. She felt a terrible *roi fainéant* there before these two, before their questioning and assessing eyes. Barbra really worked at her painting. She was quite good at it. Her little red foxes had begun to sell. Of Sasha (she forgot his other name) she knew nothing, but she could see that he was on Barbra's plane. She said slowly, meeting their assessment: 'I suppose you do everything with a terrible ardour ... I cannot....'

'Ardour is good!' Sasha looked again at Barbra and back to Liv. 'You don't, perhaps, believe in it?'

She tried to read him, and could not bring herself to take him seriously. All she said was: 'I am ... cold....' And it went on in her head that she had added the coldness to the cooking.

She was quite different from the young women he knew; they were anything but cold. She certainly looked very cool and fair sitting there in the beam of the warm sunny morning. He wanted to go on asking questions, discovering more unknown tracts in her, but was prevented by Barbra who brought the coffee.

Barbra put the tray on a little table between her and Liv. 'Tell me,' she said, curling up on the bed, 'what do you want? Don't expect a studio, nobody can find them.'

Liv did not want a studio. 'A room....'

Sasha finished it for her. 'With a gas-stove, of course.'

'Oh, that's all nonsense!' Barbra declared, smearing her *petit pain* with honey. 'I know of a nice little hotel, eighteen francs a day, and you can have your meals out.'

'I should like the gas-stove,' Liv persisted, for, of course, she meant to keep her word to her mother.

'All right, then! You shall have it! You'll forget it in about a month.... I give you exactly a month!'

'For what?'

'To forget the gas-stove!' Liv laughed, and Sasha laughed, too, but Barbra went on. 'We'll go out and get a room, and then, as it's your first day, the Place du Tertre for lunch. You'll come, Sasha?'

Liv did not listen. She was impressed by Barbra's capability. In Norway, at home in Odda, they always thought of Barbra as not good for anything except skiing and dancing and flirting. Her mother hated her, and had not wanted her to come with her. And here she was! Aunt

Sonja's place had failed. She wanted to thank Barbra. She would thank her — when Sasha wasn't there. She wished that he would go, go anywhere and put some clothes on. He seemed to know what she was thinking, for he said: 'I wish you would go.... Cook? I can't dress until you do ... can I, Barbra?'

'You could dress behind her ... she wouldn't look?'

'She would!'

'But you could take your things along to the Wilse Studio, put on your raincoat and scamper along.'

'Is it raining?' he asked Liv.

'No...' (it was really rather funny) 'but you can have my umbrella. I've finished with it!'

She breathed more easily when he had gone.

Barbra regarded her steadily, with empty, unheeding eyes. 'Are you shocked?'

'No.'

'But your mother would be!'

'So would yours!'

'No, I don't think so. She knows my views.'

Along the edge of the studio windows there trailed the dark octagonal leaves of a nasturtium, the flowers lifted tongues of flame against the dark veined leaves. 'She knows my views' fell into the flowers like a stone, a hard grey stone of decision. What really struck her as terrible was just that — the decision, the doing it deliberately and on purpose. It meant that feeling was absent. 'If you love him....'

'My dear! No more, no less, than the others! It's fatal to care.'

'That's what I do not understand.'

'Because you live in a dream. Dreams! Dreams! Medieval women eating their hearts out over their spindles, dying of desire, dying slowly, withering into death, for men who were living life to the utmost behind their backs.'

'I'm not medieval,' she said stubbornly.

'No, but you know nothing. When you wake up, you'll understand. I am only the bitter fruit of the experience of other generations of women ... the women who perished. Don't fret, Liv; I know what I am doing. I did it in Oslo, as you know. It is better to live than to die. There's nothing to be afraid of.' She drained her coffee-cup and got out of bed. Down at the end of the studio, where she had made the coffee, she filled her bath and stepped into it. There was a brisk matter-of-factness about her that paid no attention when Liv was silent. 'I've a good back ... you should see Sasha's studies.... I save him a model.... He only began last November.... Before that he was a boxer. He has a lovely body, perfect! I must show you....'

'He saves you....'

'Oh, yes, we exchange....'

It went on until she was dressed, cryptic and spasmodic, like the tiny bubbles blown when fishes rise in a lake, blown after the fish's activity, so that you knew that the fish had been there, although you did not see what it had done. Behind Barbra lay a complete scheme of achievement that was blowing little punctures into the tranquillity of Liv's mind. She had a feeling that it would go deeper, that she would know more about it, that she would be able to see down into that twilit fish world and understand it. At present Barbra was still Barbra, the girl in the Oslo school, the girl who had called the Town Engineer a sheep over the telephone.

They went out and found a room for Liv — a room with a gas-ring which Barbra said would have to do until she had got past the boiling stage. They came back and took Liv's luggage there in a taxi, unpacked a little and went to lunch at Montmartre, where Sasha joined them, then back to Montparnasse, to sit on the Dome terrace and watch a drunk Englishwoman behave like a lady. Sasha was tremendously taken with her.

'Look!' he would cry, 'there! She is going to kiss him....' They waited together for the lady to overbalance as she leaned across the table. 'There! She's done it ... and so graciously ... she is charming, charming ... but quite drunk. Isn't it marvellous? She remains a lady. It is a marvellous example of race, that! Wonderful.'

'If she weren't pretty!' Barbra shrugged her shoulders sceptically.

'It would be quite the same thing, make no difference. You can see, and the man, too!' He turned to Liv, 'The English and the Scandinavians are the worst — the women, I mean. They seem to go mad. They go further....'

Barbra interrupted, 'And fare worse!'

'I shouldn't say that,' he said.

'No, but you think it, at least we do!' She looked at Liv and got nothing. 'It's our dreadful idealism. We start off with a world that does not exist on this earth. We pay for it when we find out.'

'The obvious thing is not to find out.'

'How clever of you, Sasha! Better be debtors than fools!'

'Men,' he said smiling defeat at her, 'are always both!'

She flicked the ash off her cigarette, and her ugly broad face became tender. 'When they have come through? It is terrible, that, to fulfil every wish, to get everything, the way men do. It makes a fool of you in the end. Aren't we being philosophic?' she demanded of Liv, who did not seem to be listening.

'Showing off, I call it.' Sasha also looked at Liv.

Barbra made a resigned gesture with her hands, 'In the moon!'

And Liv, from the moon, heard them, and added her sense of hearing to her sense of vision. Faces turned and turned, and voices ran and ran, crowding and overflowing. The world is quite full of a number of people. The world is quite full of a number of people, kept ringing at the back of her mind. She was caught. 'That woman ... in red, look! What is she?'

'A Lithuanian!'

And the woman who had suddenly become a Lithuanian, leaned forward and, with a white forefinger, stroked the nose of a man in front of her. You could not tell what she was saying. It did not matter. You saw her to the roots; in bed, angry, laying a white cloth on a table, or saying, in a language that you could understand, to the fishmonger: 'I shall have three lemon soles.' You saw her as a girl of sixteen leaning out of a casement framed by clematis to watch a man with milk-cans go up a road that wound like a ribbon through meadows, you saw her in winter in thick snow-shoes, the wind whipping her pallor, and the land lying in a white sheet of heaven about her ... always beyond, something white, you wanted to draw her on a white square of paper, to listen until you heard her say yes 'a kilo of sugar', or 'soixante centimes', anything....

'That old woman who has just sat down at the table in a line with your eyes, the old woman in the chinchilla coat. She's frightfully rich.'

The spell was broken. She asked: 'What does she come here for?'

'All the young men ask for her money.'

A man with long black hair went past, a picture tucked under his arm. Sasha's shoulders went up in a hunch: 'Haydn,' he said cryptically to Barbra, and to Liv: 'Now what does he look like to you? Don't say Jesus Christ!'

'I wasn't going to. His eyebrows are too bushy.'

'What, then? ... A Galilean?'

'Yes, a fisherman.'

'One of the apostles?'

'No!'

'Your distinctions are too subtle.'

'You force me to make them.' She finished her coffee. 'Why are they all here?' she asked him dreamily.

'Everybody comes to Paris.'

It went on echoing: everybody comes to Paris. The hot September air was blocked in the spaces between the boulevards, between La Grande Chaumière and La Cigogne, between the Cigogne and the Rotonde, and between the Rotonde and them. People moved like sedimentary particles at the bottom of it. Little tired and vivid people, full of egotism. Was not a man shouting in an American voice: 'You can't beat me. You can't beat me.' No, they could not be beaten. They were human beings, lords of creation, they spun pictures and poems. They were greater than animals. Two girls with identical complexions came up and spoke to Barbra and Sasha, and were introduced — Irma and Geneviève. They stared, and then took no more notice of her. She was content with their names. Geneviève meant Paris to her — grey streets spiked with churches, the hill at Montmartre, the river, the fine old chiselled houses. Old and grey, old and grey, centuries written into the lines. This was her first day in Paris. There was born in her a great tenderness, like hope when it quickens from slumber, a release, a catch of the breath at the start of a race, a tremor, and in a moment she was in the thrall of Paris, the thrall that accepts everything, everything because it is human — like the crowd about her. The quality of Paris is not strained....

'We will go to Bagatelle, and this evening we are going to take you to Fuller's studio.... Hello! There's Inger Wilse and her brother, the tall girl who is with them is a dancer....'

Liv was meshed in a positive whirl of introductions and recognitions, of changing tables, of a blond god eating an ice, of a tray of fruit carried head-high above them, and the scream of trams....

Chapter Four

She arrived at the Fuller studio at half-past nine. Barbra had said 'be late' and she was early. She hesitated, then rang the bell. She was in one of her moods, like the mood in which she had left Odda. Her soul seemed to be striding away from her, making fine gestures of dis-embarrassment, as of a fleet runner parting branches and clearing her paths. She was exalted as she had been exalted going through the Sorfjorden, lifted out of herself, separated, so that she saw things and actions and people as through special purple rays, wherein particles of their meanings danced and became significant. She could have drawn them as a physician draws the germ of a disease, given them form.

The door opened and through parted curtains the studio spun away from her in a mesh of soft reds and yellows. There was a group at the far end composed of a young woman, rising from a divan like a hyacinth from an ochre pot; the blond god who had been at the Dome (she knew him at once); a girl in a white shawl with lips slashed into a face that matched the shawl, and dark, parted hair; a broad, husky-voiced man in a beige suit, who was her host — Jacob Fuller — for he was coming towards her. She put out her hand and as she put out her hand the mood tormented her, swelled in her like a tide. She stood, battling with it into a blindness in which she was conscious of one man behind the group. Nobody could avoid seeing him, he was taller than the others, more distinguished, but it was neither his height nor his distinction that drew her and blinded her to the others. She was conscious of him with the full prescience of the mood that was upon her, so that her first sight of him became a mere recognition. He was no stranger to her like Sasha. She could have gone up to him where he was standing beside the horrible statue and greeted him as one she had known ... oh, when was it? It was like standing on the steps, that first time, with Aunt Sonja, the midnatssol burning over the fjelds and trees. It was odd how she thought of Aunt Sonja and wanted, quick as a flash, to write to her about this stranger. A birch had stood out, fine and straight and solitary, holding up a plume of feathers against the sky, standing very still, like this stranger. She told her name to Jacob Fuller, her voice coming from far off, proclaiming her identity like a flag on a kopje, waving its ownership in some wilderness of the earth: 'I am Liv Evensen. Barbra Grondahl told me to come.'

'Liv! Liv!' Jacob Fuller's husky, American drawl repeated it, pronouncing it like the leaf of a tree, 'falling leaves....'

The group was listening. 'It means Life,' she said in English. She never moved. She was frozen against them, all her senses gathered like faggots for the lighting against this man. She did not look at him, but she knew that, like the others, he was looking at her. She was introduced to the hyacinth woman by her host. She was Mrs Fuller. Mina Fuller, for the girl in the shawl said with the same hard scrutiny in her eyes as Sasha had when he said she was paintable, 'Mina thinks that you are extraordinary.'

'But no...' she found the English very difficult, and lapsed into French, 'I am Norwegian.' She knew that she had been foolish, that she had nationalised the extraordinariness, but she felt calm, unmoved, icy about their opinion. What did it matter?

Mrs Fuller asked her what she was doing — 'painting like Barbra Grondahl?'

'No. I have come to Paris ... to study cooking!'

Jacob Fuller's shoulders heaved with muted laughter. She was aware that he was laughing, but the laughter was unheard. She looked at him wonderingly, the trick revealing him to her somehow as a man ready for impulses, knowing how to deal with them. He knew how not to laugh out loud.

'There!' declared Mrs Fuller, 'what did I say?'

'Here,' said Jacob Fuller, 'you must have a cocktail!'

'I prefer an ice,' she said, and looked at the tall man behind Mrs Fuller.

'I will get you one,' he said instantly, and crossed behind the girl in the shawl, who turned her head in profile and said to him, 'and me, too?'

'Have you already had one — a cocktail?' Mrs Fuller asked.

She shook her head.

'Then you ought to, just to get on our level.'

'No,' Jacob Fuller sank down on the divan beside his wife, 'leave her alone, she is all right as it is.' He explained it to her, leaning forward and touching the arm of her chair with a soft, brownish hand, 'the world seen through a cocktail is veiled, like the houris in paradise, you can bear it, you feel that it is very pleasant, and may become more so, and your wits are wonderful, wonderful.' He slid from the definition into a confidence, 'I want very much to write a novel where the chapters shall be degrees of intoxication.'

'Oh, but Jacob, all novels are that already!'

'"Drunk with love!" Here' — he turned to Liv — 'is Per Malom with your ices!'

Per Malom! Per Malom! The name sang out, each separate letter a chime. Yes, she would write to Aunt Sonja. She had posted her letters. She had written to them all, even Uncle Johan had had a card, but to Aunt Sonja she had not written. He gave her her ice, steadying it, while she took it from him, with long, chiselled fingers. She saw the lines on his knuckles etched and clear. She raised her eyes and thanked him. The acknowledgement passed between them, a necessary ritual. He bowed and passed from her, another ritual. Jacob Fuller was a sculptor. Barbra had said he hacked beasts out of marble. There was a lamb lying on a pedestal behind him, quite dead, drooping with that limpness that is not yet cold, perfectly pliant, as though it had been boned, the fleece was cut like flakes. He saw her looking at it and made her get up to examine it with him, explaining that he had a passion for doing lambs. 'My father was a Kosher butcher, and, as a small boy, I used to see these lambs.' She liked him very much when he told her that, and it gave her some clue to his laughter. 'They used to hang like that; you'd think they hadn't yet been born. People jeer at me for doing lambs ... there have been so many Christian lambs, Goy lambs, Miss Evensen, lambs in the bosom, carried through snowstorms, and none of them a real lamb, killed to match the peas....' He stroked the marble caressingly. 'They lie like that ... that's a real Blakey lamb, a real lovely innocent little thing, with the fleece melting on it straight out of its mother's womb ... then hardened, chilled by death....'

'Fuller, you are a wonderful showman, you'd convince anybody!' Per Malom said over her shoulder.

'Have I convinced you?' he asked.

'No. We think in different mediums.'

'He talks like a poet.' She turned and said it directly into Per Malom's face.

He smiled at her and went away from her to Mina Fuller. She saw him talking to Mina Fuller with animation, and, as though he were persuading her about something. He appeared to have moved from her into Mina Fuller's world, and she was left derelict, no longer interested in Jacob Fuller's lamb.

Mina was saying to him, looking up at him with that arch sweetness that preserved her from being grown up: 'Another conquest, Per?'

'Why, yes!'

'Be careful. She is ... oh, remote!'

'So near, and yet so far ... a cook!' They enjoyed the joke together.

'One day, Per, you will get caught.'

'Never, now. I am — no longer snareable,' he added, 'I have escaped from the fowler.'

'Ever since....'

'Don't,' he said, 'mention Tana Talladra's name,' and mentioned it himself. He had a swift, piercing image of a Spanish girl in a white, billowy frock, he heard her laughter. To his dying day he would be able to see her in that frock and hear that laughter. It would torment him as long as he lived. She had laughed at him, fooled him, trailed a snake through the white roses of his worship. Women were to him, since that episode, like transparent spheres of glass, which he could take in his hands and fondle and caress as he wished, read what he wished into the crystal, and then drop it, smash into a million pieces, into the white roses that he had given Tana Talladra. Mina went away from him to greet some newcomers. He saw the strong Barbra Grondahl come in with the boy Sasha — Sasha's latest. The boy looked gentle beside Barbra, a dark reed. 'Women,' he thought, 'are so much more brutal than men, they have the instincts of animals.' Barbra had a trick of moving her shoulder blades that reminded him of a filly in the Andorras. The English newcomers were making a great clatter of tongues, he wished the English could learn to pitch their voices in a lower key when they got excited. If you did not know English it sounded terrible like a day in the market, a winter market, full of geese.

Sasha went up to Liv and began to tell her who people were.

She waited for him to come to Per Malom. He went to everybody else, telling her minute details that established them in frames in her cognition of them. The girl in the white shawl (she did not catch her name) was a dancer. Jacob Fuller was a Jew. He had told her that himself when he had said his father was a Kosher butcher ... a little dark man in a blue-striped apron sharpening a knife ... white Leghorns running about without heads. She liked Jacob Fuller. He was real. There was no pretence about him, he loved his lambs. He gave her a sense of breadth. Sasha was still cataloguing the people in the room. He did not mention Per Malom. 'Why,' she asked, 'do you not tell me about Per Malom?'

'Because you wanted to know.'

That was a lie, because he could not have known. She had given him no sign. It was true, of course, that she did want to know, but a lie for him to know it. She denied it, feeling like the apostle Peter listening to the cock crow.

'You need not pretend. Every new girl asks about him, falls in love with him; I warn you!'

He was truly in earnest, with an air of trying to save her. 'You need have no fear!' she said, and instantly remembered Harald Christensen. She held up her hand with the ring on it, and treble, treble, treble the cock crew, and she felt the apostle Peter inside her.

'Oh, that's nothing!'

'It depends…' she tried to bastion it as a defence and gave it up. 'Tell me … what is he?'

'A painter. Have you never heard of him?'

'No, I have never heard of him. In Norway we hear very little.'

'His mother was a Norwegian, his father a Spaniard. He has the ice of one and the vice of the other … hot and cold.'

He was Norwegian. He would be able to speak her language. It warmed her like a cloak thrown suddenly about her, brought them closer. And, as though the fact had become manifest, he was there beside her, ready to speak to her. She wished that Sasha would go away and leave them, and immediately wished him to stay, because it did not matter whether he was there or not. She felt an intense calmness like strength. It made her at ease with him. In some sense it sprang from him and pervaded her. 'I hear,' she looked at him, her expression serious and with a certain fatigue in it, 'that you are Norwegian?'

'My mother, yes. I have never been there. I was brought up in Spain. I am afraid that I am quite out of sympathy with your country.'

'Why?' She asked it naturally.

He hesitated, as though measuring the limit to which he could go, and went as far as possible. 'The Norwegian character strikes me as so fluent, running out, no stability.... You are all dreams, you have never recovered from your first adventure, as a race or individually!'

She was frowning, trying to comprehend. 'You mean — the Vikings?'

'The Vikings, if you like.'

'Oh,' she cried, exasperated with her inability to understand him, 'what do you mean?'

'Let me put it like this, and mind you, I have a right' (he meant his mother) 'to say it, you have the easy-flowing characteristics of an early people, the going out, the grand adventure, you did it perfectly once ... and then never again, never again like that. To make a habit of perfection is to cheat it.... You are like that as a race and individually.'

'You mean that we are narrow — limited?'

'Exactly.' His smile contradicted the words.

He wasn't in earnest. But in her heart she knew that he had touched some fragment of the truth, and blurred it, blurred it perhaps because he had hated his father, or had loved his mother too much. She asked: 'And isn't it worth it — one grand adventure?' she repeated his words.

'There is never one. There are hundreds and hundreds.'

They became multiplied for her. The world spawned with adventures, and floated out like the old ships from the North

Sea to the Pacific. 'And all together, at the end, they make one…'
she teased him, not kittenishly, but as his equal, 'grand adventure.'

'You are very young to talk like that.'

What had youth to do with it? Aunt Sonja would never have
said that. She would have said nothing. Her aunt was not afraid
of dreams. She wanted to tell him about Aunt Sonja, to make
him see her aunt's life up there in the Rindalsholm valley, and
by the time that she sought for words and found them her
thoughts had strayed from Rindalsholm to Sulitelma, to the
silted copper, and Astrid leaning down with Erik to feel the ore
which lay heavy as bronze and dark as blood on the mountain.
There was no use in trying if he had never been there. He
would know nothing of her land until he had been there. He
thought that they were stuffed with dreams. For Aunt Sonja
the dreams were the reality, and Aunt Sonja neglected
nothing. She looked down the room at the chattering throng,
and said, spiked to say it: 'Do you call this real?'

'Very!'

She felt outside it suddenly, detached as she had been
when she had entered, separated. The blond god came up to
her, accompanied by Barbra, and a small, neat man with a
red beard. The god was Austrian — Rudolf Flesche. He and
Barbra had brought the red-bearded man to Per Malom for
judgment. Barbra's eyes were loaded and glazed. She spoke
as though every word dragged a weight, looking all the time
at Per Malom with strange persistence, as though he
magnetised her. She was like a pigeon before a serpent, and
like the serpent he was indifferent.

'Poor Pol, pretty Pol … he can't keep his mistresses…. It is
getting quite expensive.'

'Give them up,' said Per Malom. He was standing beside Liv, a little behind so that she could not see his face. She felt him as a dark presence, unsmiling, above her.

The red-bearded man shrugged his shoulders and his hands struck out vigorously. 'I can't! It ruins my work. I...' he was glowing up at Per Malom like a lighted coal, 'I am *un homme positif!*

The blond god chuckled and turned to Liv. 'He is a mathematical painter ... trigonometry, geometry ... you know!' She did not know, but she listened.

'Then why?' Per Malom moved one foot behind the other.

'It's not me! It's the mice. They can't stand the mice.'

'The mistresses cost him so much that he cannot afford mousetraps. He has invented a method. He has stretched a line across like a telegraph wire, with pieces of cheese along it at intervals like the Morse code. The mice walk the tight rope and drop into basins of water provided for them. It seems they squeal horribly and make a dreadful struggle, and no girl can stand it. They sit up and beg him to rescue the creatures.'

'And when I rescue an occasional one, to keep them quiet, they squeal worse than the mice. Ugh! It gets on one's nerves.'

'Why not change the studio?' Liv was rash enough to suggest, and was met by a chorus of disapproval, and the information that as the studio cost him only two hundred francs a month, and he had no money, he would be a fool to give it up.

'Sasha says he ought to search until he finds a woman from the Caucasus. They can stand anything.'

'Yes,' said Per Malom, 'it appears to be the only thing to do.' The tone of his voice dismissed them and they went away. He sat down again beside Liv. He leaned towards her with his elbow on his knee and his chin on his hand. His face had a rare quality of warmth in it, a glow as of hidden heat, but his manner was deadly calm and cold, and his voice matched it. 'That,' he emphasised it, 'is not Paris!'

'I am not mistaking it,' she said, with something of his own quietness. They exchanged a deep look.

'Sometimes,' he went on, 'I wonder why I stay here.'

She was silent. She felt like saying: 'I wonder why I have come.' But she was more curious about him. She wanted to know something of his background and did not dare to ask.

He was reading her, and finding something that eluded him. He thought: 'She is the sort that will give everything or nothing.'

'You know, of course, that you are very beautiful?'

She turned her face slowly away from him, then slowly back again and said nothing. She felt as though he had struck her.

'Forgive me!' he pleaded, conscious that he ought not to have said what he had said.

She was at ease again, forgiving him completely because he had understood that he had embarrassed her. And behind him she sensed a life that was entirely hidden from her, but which had made him what he was, intimate to her, with that same clairvoyance that had given her Aunt Sonja before Aunt Sonja had withdrawn herself. The withdrawal did not matter. Nothing could be taken back from that intimacy. It endured. In the centre of the room she saw Barbra by the piano with the girl in the shawl. The girl in the shawl was going to sing.

As if he saw into her mind, he said: 'There are some things that are known, nothing creates them, we touch them — out in blind space — and they are there!'

'Yes, yes.' She was harassed by his comprehension, and wanted to hide from it. It unsteadied her, frightened her. Behind his words she recollected her father brooding over the gaily-coloured congregation, and declaring unto them with a sort of prophecy — before her time came, she brought forth! What had the text got to do with it? Her father laid the book down on the sampler of Isaac and his flock, laid the book down on the tiny, tiny *petits points* of Isaac and his flock. She was so calm underneath, so still, taking long breaths.

'Paris,' he was saying to her, 'is an eternal mother, drawing us to her knees. She knows everything that there is to know. We can shock her by no confession. Her kings taught her, her cardinals, her courtesans. She has no shams.'

'It is not good to pretend,' she said simply, as though he were giving her a lesson. She spread one hand on her knee and placed the other on top of it. She felt Fru Christensen's ring. The hand on top tightened over the ring and concealed it.

'In this room,' he said, 'we are all foreigners. We have the behaviour of foreigners. We are in Paris and not of it, although Paris is of us ... although never in us!' He smiled.

She smiled too, taking light from him. She felt extraordinarily happy, full with happiness. Above them, above the voices that enveloped them, there rose Solveig's song. She leaned forward, her eyes rapt. 'Listen!' The voice on the mountain. There came over her a magic loneliness, and the wheel of wings in a vast solitude, the wild, clean eyes of eagles, bare crags, and the deep plunge of water, and a man lost amongst all these things, a man for whom that voice was crying. A man crying amongst the earthly mountains. It was almost too much for her to sit there, hiding herself outwardly, containing these wild and galloping thoughts and saving her secrecy. She felt that Per Malom knew the wildness that was going on inside her, that from him nothing was hidden. It kept her from looking at him, from moving, lest a touch would frustrate all that guarded her. He became for her Per Gynt, Everyman, and she saw him with his mother and with Solveig, the bombast of achievement dropping away from him, leaving him to be pitied....

The song dropped and died. The girl in the white shawl stood up and looked around, the miracle still transfusing her, so that Liv wanted to cry out to her: 'Don't look! Don't let them see!'

'Barbra Grondahl asked her to sing that!'

'I suppose so,' she said, and her breath went out like a ghost.

'It wasn't worth it ... for these.' He indicated the crowd of people. 'Mina Fuller's crowd.' Many more had come in, so that one lost count of the ones one knew.

'Oh, but how do you know?' she asked, pleading for a wider sympathy.

He said nothing. She was foolish to have asked that, to turn the compliment that he was giving her. It made her faulty, sent him, in spite of himself, to the vision of Tana Talladra, with whom he compared all women — and found them wanting. Dark Tana in a white gauze dress that blew her into a rose. Tana — flushed and dark and holy and profane. Tana was cruel. She loved power. She had begun early and she hated men, hated them until she hurt and wounded them, wounded them till they died and perished and dried and were of no more use, and then she was appeased. She was like a goddess to whom one sacrificed the goats. She was in Toledo. She would escape from her dreadful husband to go and sit with his mother. They would talk about him and make a mock of him. They did not even understand his pictures. It took mad Rahel to do that, and that added to the irony.

'I mean,' Liv covered her error, 'that if it … reached only one, and how do you know? It was worth it.'

'One … or two.' His eyes united them.

And this time she had the sense to be silent.

He stood up suddenly, aware that Olga Wienawski would be certain to sing some platitude like the Volga boat-song. In any case, he hated encores. Once was always enough. The red-bearded man approached a little table close to them, snatched an ash tray and darted away from them. 'Poor Pol Parrot!'

'His name isn't really that?' she asked.

'It really is.' His eyes were lit again. He looked from her to Pol Parrot. 'An *homme positif!* My God!'

He summarised for her all the positive men of the world.

'It is his favourite phrase. He copied it from some Pole.'

She stood up beside him, expressing thereby subtly and unwittingly her union with his mood.

It made him say to her: 'Shall we go? You can come back if you want to, but it is very quiet in the street, shall we walk down the rue des Petits Champs and back again?'

She was conscious of all the eyes upon them as they passed out of the room. Jacob Fuller made an attempt to come towards them, but Per Malom waved him away. Olga Wienawski was beginning to sing — the slow, deadly Volga poison of patience. She always sang that. It suited her voice. There was in it for him the drone of slavery. He had heard

Russians sing it, and it had been spoiled for him for ever by the throaty rasp of a woman who was a tyrant, a woman who boasted of her friendship with the Tsar, and sent her daughter, who had been educated in the institute for the daughters of noblemen in St Petersburg to a café on the *quais* to earn what she could, and turned her son into a *gigolo*. She coached him deliberately to capture the purses of rich American women, who had to pay for love. It was quiet in the street, the air was soft and refreshing. The branches of trees fell in green shadows over a wall. 'What are you going to do?' he asked abruptly, stopping for a pace in the spill of light from an electric lamp.

She understand perfectly that he was asking her into time and the future, that he did not mean immediately, and yet she said, to gain her wits for herself: 'I shall try to get cooking lessons.'

She did not see his smile. 'I must try to find you a cook.'

'If you could I should be very grateful.' Her words felt hollow. Yet what was she to say to him? They walked to the end of the street in silence. She was in Paris and she was exquisitely happy. She loved and forgave everybody. The houses were foreign to her, cold and so close together, and then separated by trees, by gardens. And over the roofs the sky was shaded like an Etruscan vase, from jade to violet. Slits of lemon-coloured light shone through passing *persiennes*. People passed her with bright eyes. She would have liked to have shown him how happy she was, to have folded her hands and cried out to him, before him: 'I am in Paris and I am happy! I have always, always wanted to come. I have always wanted to … get away.' It was quite fitting that he should stop, and, looking straight into her eyes, ask her:

'Leaving the cooking out of it ... what are you going to do with yourself?'

'That...' she hesitated, and then was truthful, 'I can't tell you ... not yet!'

He repeated it. 'Not yet!'

'I have always wanted to come.'

'That is nothing ... the fledgling's flight. We are never ourselves until we go away. We have to escape.'

'It is an escape?' She made a question of it, and remembered Harald Christensen.

'From shelter, from all that can protect us from danger, from courage, even....' He had to reveal it to her, to save her from hardening against him, as though his sex protected him in a special manner (and he thought of the young man who had been turned by his mother into a *gigolo*) 'for men it is that ... a plunge into danger. The thing is to be fearless....' He was a sorry master to be teaching her that, he, whose courage had been like a million shields and had saved him from nothing. He was strictly derived from his mother who had given his father more than he had been able to take. She had been starved, and he had had to pay for her hunger. His nature paid. It was good for his work. It gave him the artist's distortion. 'You must come to see my pictures.'

It was, to her, in that moment, that he invited her into his life. His voice came to her from his hidden thoughts, from the dark places where he remained secret, and bade her come in. She felt powerless against him, against the moment. After a pause, she said: 'I will come.'

They walked past the studio entrance and returned to it. He paused. He was not going back into Mina Fuller's crowd.

'You must ask Barbra Grondahl to bring you,' he said, and held out his hand.

She went back after he had left her, and stood between the parted curtains, looking on. They were dancing, and Sasha was at the piano playing a mad music that set her blood on fire. Jacob Fuller, with the singing girl in his grasp, moved like a Trold. Beyond them all she felt that Hulder was there with her beautiful face, bewitching them, and wagging a tail that went for miles and miles in great coils ready to ensnare them. The Austrian boy came up to her and asked her to dance, saying: 'We ought to, we're both fair, we'd go well together.'

Immediately he asked her to dance she felt that she could not. 'I am too tired to dance.' She saw his disappointment, and added, solely to appease him: 'I have been up since half-past three in the morning.'

'When most of us are going to bed.'

She was not tired, at least she did not feel tired; she began to analyse her motive for giving him that answer, and knew that if Per Malom had asked her to dance with him that she would not have refused. It made her go hot inside. Yet it was true. She did not want to dance with anybody but Per Malom. This boy was good enough looking. If she could refuse him she could refuse anybody. She would not have refused Per Malom. 'And the night before I was on the sea, coming from Norway!'

'Then you must be tired.' He believed her at last.

Only such a short time since she had watched the last speck of Norway disappear. It seemed years and years since ... since she had met Per Malom. She stood between the parted curtains, dazzled and bewildered, belonging neither to Norway nor to here, belonging, it seemed, no longer to herself ... belonging to nobody, she argued, just to preserve her reason.

Jacob Fuller, seeing her, said to Olga: 'She knows how to pose, that new girl.'

'I thought she went away with Per Malom,' Olga remarked with drowsy eyes, the rhythm of the dance in her senses.

'She has come back.'

They exchanged a look. At the end of the dance Jacob Fuller sought Liv, who had moved away from the curtains. She had gone back to where she had been sitting with Per Malom. She made a place for him. 'Are you enjoying yourself?' he asked in his frank, kind way.

'Very much.'

'Not tired?'

'No.'

He lit a cigarette. 'What do you think of him ... do you like him?'

He was going too far to ask her that. She stiffened and was defeated by his expression. He did not seem to expect her to reply, for he added, sheltering the flame of a second match in the cup of his hand: 'Queer fellow, Malom. Queer. Unhappy.'

She absorbed this clue to him, and was silent. Everything that she might or could hear about him merely corroborated what her instincts already told her. The first mention of anything about him made her curious, and immediately she knew what it was, she felt that it was of no significance. Jacob Fuller was smiling at her out of his kind black eyes. She liked Jacob Fuller, liked him tremendously. There was a deep black

warmth about him, like a dark ram. She smiled back at him.
'I think, after all, that I would like to go back to my hotel'
(she had almost said 'home', and was pulled up by the liberty
of the word; later on she might be able to use it). Mina Fuller
said, repeating what her husband had said half-a-dozen times:
'You will come again? You will come?' She promised that she
would come. Mina Fuller glinted up at her like a blue flower
with that bright, dazed gleam in her eyes that was to be seen in
most of the other eyes in the room: 'You are quite a sensation!'

She did not feel that she was a sensation, but that something very sensational had happened to her. She went away
from them feeling that she had peered into another planet —
that she had, perhaps, gone through the *midnatssol* into a
world of strange lights and colours, where people were agitated
for different reasons than in the world which she knew.

When she asked Barbra Grondahl to take her to Per
Malom's studio Barbra laughed, a peculiar, informed laugh,
that had a syntax utterly outside her means of interpreting it.
She waited for a refusal, and none came. Barbra said nothing
at all. She could not ask her again. It would look too much
like pleading. She was forced into the silence which was set
by Barbra's manner. And when, one day when they were
talking about painting, and Per Malom's name had been
mentioned, she asked Sasha, he also laughed and said
nothing. She went several times to the Fullers' without
meeting him again.

Three weeks after their first meeting he came himself to
see her. She had taken down a letter from the hotel rack and
was deep in her mother's regrets that she had not gone to
Roger Sigmundson at the Legation, with her difficulty about

Aunt Sonja's hotel, instead of going to Barbra Grondahl. She was smiling, with the letter in her hand, over the idea of going to the Legation about the *punaises* and the Russian general, when his voice said at her side:

'I have found you.' He saw the smile melt into her and remain in her. She did not turn immediately.

'Yes,' she answered stupidly.

He relieved her. He said: 'I have found you a cook!'

'How kind of you! But I have already begun. I have begun with sauces.' What foolish things she was saying to him! It was like standing on the opposite bank of a river, shouting nonsense across, and a wind blowing so hard that nothing mattered. The osiers were bent double, and the trees wracked and swept, and the water so turbulent and muddied that you could not see to the bottom of it, and all sorts of things were carried away.

'I have been waiting for you to come to see my pictures.'

'I meant to come.'

'But you have not come!'

She gave him the bare truth: 'I do not know where your studio is.'

'I will take you there. I will take you there now, if you want to.'

'Yes,' she said, 'I will go with you.'

It was as simple as that. She went along a few streets with him, seeing an old woman with a hare in a basket, a house signed 'Jules Casselan', and two tiny children under a minute parasol. But it was a whole voyage to her in her spirit — longer than from Odda to Sulitelma, from Sulitelma to Bodo, to Bordeaux. She travelled from childhood (from the stockings that were taped on to her stays), from the day that Fru Christensen fastened her hair up with tortoiseshell pins and sent her home to her mother, to the moment after her father's funeral, when her mother announced the visit to Aunt Sonja. There were roses in the Hardanger garden and Harald Christensen said that he would wait until he got her. It was far away, far away, shut into a disc of distance like the Danish governess's portrait of herself with a story-book on her knee. The flat book with the wide white margins lay open on her knee, and her hair was very curly, and just down to her shoulders ... it went long when you wet it and combed it out, and the nails on her fingers were very badly painted. The white of her pinafore was the same as the white of the margins, and the ugly duckling in the picture was painted upside down so that you had to turn the portrait round to see it....

The studio was in the street behind the Fullers'. She had passed it every time that she had been to them. Her heart was thumping as he unlocked the door for her.

He shut the door and watched her go straight down the full length of the room to the window that was open against the boughs of an acacia. The tree made a screen at that side of the window, and, as she stood there, a faded green light was filtered through and she was transfigured by it. She stood in a deep cool sea of light, as she turned to him, looking at him with her steady, unequivocal eyes. She was different from every other girl that he had known. He experienced a strange kinship with her. She would never let him down. There was no artifice about her, none of those tricks that are supposed to be womanly and are the mere relics of the age in the jungle. He joined her, and together they looked out into the screen of the acacia. 'I knew you would come.' He had a sense of fate with her. He had had a sense of fate with Tana. Long ago he had said to Tana: 'I knew you would come', and Tana had bowed low to him, her dress going out like petals, and the shadows of the twilight had run between her bosoms as her laughter ran into his soul. This girl did not laugh. She was silent. She was cold and contained as a glacier. He felt cruel towards her, seared through and through by the memory of Tana Talladra. 'Did you hear?' he asked.

'Yes,' her voice was dry, drawn from her, 'I knew, too.'

'Liv!' he cried her name, and forced her to look at him. She felt his will and resisted it. She did not look. 'What are we going to do about it?' he asked. She was so still, so aloof, that his eyes had full freedom. The cheek against her mouth was lovely. She was so young that she knew how to resist him. He waited.

She turned then, and her hands broke into a gesture as she moved away from him. 'Show me the pictures,' she said. The resistance passed from her to him, and they were back again to where they had been in the street, before they had reached his studio, before he had shut the door. He smiled to himself. It was a knight's move and he loved her for it. She was no spendthrift.

And in her it had gone down in a pure shaft of pain. She felt the sweetness of pain, the submission. She was chastened into a queer dignity that gave sorrow to her eyes and mouth. It made her slow with him, gathering everything that she might do before him as though it were precious. She could not help feeling like that. It had descended upon her, like her pity for Aunt Sonja. It was comprehension of something so great that she was humbled before it and yet filled with a devastating pride. Once, long ago, when she had hung the Christmas sheaf out from the door-post for the winter birds, she had experienced lavishness and tenderness that was like this. She had felt it watching the tiny starved birds fluttering in the frost then alighting on the sheaf that she had put out for them in remembrance of Christ who had been born in a stable.

'Do you know anything about painting?' he asked.

'Nothing ... except what we were taught long ago by our governess.'

'Then why do you want to see my pictures?'

She did not answer. He watched the confusion running through her and back as in a tide. He tormented her.

'Because they are mine?'

She raised her eyes, pleading against him. She looked away again and said: 'Yes.' There was no use hiding it. It could not be hidden. It needed no speech to betray it.

Her directness turned in him, made him subtle with her, eager to darken the clear stream of her mind. He said, lightly, as though it made the present moment casual, 'I've shown them to heaps of other girls.'

'Why, of course,' she said, relieved, as though he had been withdrawn from her. Sasha had said: 'Every new girl falls in love with him.' It meant nothing to him. And immediately she believed that, she denied it, for she knew that what she was feeling he was feeling too. It was there. It wove them together. It shut out the world as it had shut out the crowd at Mina Fuller's.

'Liv!' he cried, 'you are a wonderful girl! You are so extra- ordinarily honest. Tell me, what would you do if you loved a man and he didn't want you?'

She locked her fingers together and kept her eyes on the pictures that he was taking out from a group of others on the floor against the wall. She did not answer. Fru Christensen's ring was there. He was showing her a street in Toledo, with the cathedral in the background, and then the portrait of a girl in a white frock, a Spanish girl with a rose in her hair, a girl with beautiful hands and arms. Her face was in profile, dark and lovely as the rose in her hair. She was transfigured in the painting by light, translucent, as though she stood in sunlight. She praised her beauty, and as soon as she began to do so he turned the picture away and showed her another of a potter's shop, and immediately afterwards he said: 'And now, no more. You must look round the walls!'

She did not look, beyond a cursory glance, at the pictures that were hung on the walls. She went back to the window, drawn by the coolness of the green tree, and she thought: I must go now. I must go. There is nothing to stay for.

'What are you thinking of?' he asked, beside her again.

'That I must go.'

He leaned against the window-pane, conscious not of her, but of Tana. Tana had said, too: 'I must go.' God! They were all alike. They had one purpose. It had taken Tana three years to say that she must go, but she had gone. In the end she had gone. She had taken the best part of his life with her. He had travelled in order to escape the ache that she had left. It was still there. He gazed out at the dark incised bark of the tree, thinking of the waste that women had the power to inflict on men's lives. Since Tana, every woman had been a means of revenge to him. 'Tell me, Liv, what do you know of men? ... beyond your father, of course!' He knew that she was without experience, the sort of experience that teaches women to play with men. She had no wiles.

'My father died in the summer ... and...' she held up her hand with the ring, 'Harald Christensen.'

'You are going to marry him?'

She was silent. She was remembering that Aunt Sonja had said that she was never to let herself forget Harald Christensen.

'Has he kissed you?'

'Yes.' She went tense, leaning forward towards the window.

'How?' His head was very close to hers. She could feel his breath on her cheek. His arm went round her. She stood up within the fold of his arm, very erect, facing him. And, as though the rising of her will gave him power over her, he drew her towards him. 'Liv ... give in. It's useless.'

'Oh, oh!' she cried. She knew it was useless.

Her head drooped back like a flower on a stalk. He took her face in his two hands and kissed her. 'Beautiful thing! Beautiful thing!' She was a delight to him. 'It wasn't like that?'

No, no! It hadn't been like that. A bee droned in the window-space, hovered and went out again. She released herself from his arms, put her hand on the window, and leaned her cheek against it and stared out into the dark depths of the tree. Across the garden a glass roof was spread out in grey-green squares like lichen and at its edge waved branches of a tamarisk. She saw these things, merely perceived that they were there. She felt nothing towards or about them, nothing towards or about anything except that she was there by the side of Per Malom, that she had been in his arms, that he had kissed her. He was there beside her, and they were united in the silence, belonging to each other. The tranquillity was a force to her. In it her consciousness seemed to beat with a thousand beats into a rhythm that she had never before known, and to declare to her that this was the meaning of life. It was as when the deaf hear amidst a million hammers. Everything that had ever been beautiful to her, every moment, was reaped and given into her hands. She was Ruth before Boaz … ready for tears amidst the stranger's grain....

He had no wish to shatter the spell. He, too, was held in it. It gave him balm. There was, in this girl a simplicity, a directness that ran like water in the desert that Tana had made of his soul. He was quickened by her, by her stillness. She took him with her into her own far Northern spirit, and he was bleached out there in her white snows and exalted. It made him wonder if his Norse blood, the blood that came from his mother's people, was responding to her. His mother had said to him once, revealing her starvation: 'In the South you love with the body, in the North we love with our souls!' He had laughed at her, because he was young then, and in love with Tana. Now, in this moment, he began to understand his mother. He began to understand that bitterness that made her alien in Spain, unhappy, the scorn with which she said such things as: 'Our flowers are intenser than yours, the colours … you can't imagine them! We only have the sun for a little while, a little while, but how we worship it! We open our doors and windows, our fields, our hearts, we drink it in....'

'Some day,' he said slowly, 'I shall go to Norway.'

And she answered, as though from the future rather than from the present: 'Perhaps when you come, you will stay!'

'Perhaps!' He saw humanity making the same journey, and it became significant of the journey from youth to age. The North was very old and calm, hoar with winters, beautiful as the old are beautiful, by the dignity of living, triumphant over danger.

'Your mother,' she asked. 'Has she never gone back?'

'Never. She is beyond persuasion. It is very strange. You feel ... she makes you feel her intense love for her country, and whenever you suggest that she might like to visit it again, she rises, positively rises against you as though you had suggested a sacrilege....'

'Why is that?' She was looking at him, and thinking of his mother.

'It is very queer. I do not understand it. She is — I think that she is afraid....'

'Afraid!'

'She might not want to come back.'

'Then she is not happy!'

'No,' he repeated, marvelling how she could pierce through the scraps that he was showing her of his mother's personality, 'she is not happy.' The sympathy in her eyes was genuine.

His mother was in Spain and she was not happy. Jacob Fuller had said: 'He is unhappy.' It emptied, for her, some stability in them, some lack of knowing what happiness was, perhaps? She was not sure. She did not herself know what happiness was. A moment ago she had known rapture, but it was not happiness. There was too much pain in it, too much bliss.... 'Oh, dear!' she cried, 'what is it?'

'What is what?' he put his arm about her again, and his voice was tender.

'Happiness.' She did not resist him. She did not feel that she wanted to resist him.

'Isn't it this?' He made her look at him.

She looked back steadily and shook her head. She felt too great with feeling to be happy.

He put his other arm round her and his hands slipped up on her shoulders, and he drew her closer. He found himself wishing, with a force that was almost blame of Tana, that he had met her at the beginning, before any of them, before Tana. She would never have wrecked him. He was stabbed by a swift realisation that he could reach in her heights of love that he had never dreamt of. She had, he was aware, some gift that appeased his nature such as no other woman. 'Liv ... we ought to have met long ago.'

'I feel that we have.'

'That we belong to each other?'

She nodded. That first moment, beyond the approaching Jacob Fuller, she had been conscious of him terribly. It was like waiting for the tide to come in, and then for it to come in so swiftly and with such a flow that you were caught and taken by it.

Quite suddenly he let her go and began to walk up and down the room.

She watched him. For the first time he was a stranger, lost to her. He reminded her of Harald Christensen coming up to the house and refusing to come in. And, as if she added him on to her own problem with Harald Christensen, she found herself asking him: 'What are you going to do?'

He was right at the other end when he stopped and stared at her. She amazed him. She had that quality of action which he had always wanted in women, the certainty of knowing where she was going to. She did not leave all the responsibility to him. There was no weakness, no pretence of weakness about her, and yet, she was gentler than any of them. She was passionate and clear. There was no flickering of frail flames about her. As she stood there, asking him so simply what he was going to do, she had an air of accepting all his entanglements and telling him to get clear of them. 'You see, Liv,' he said, telling her what he felt sure she knew already, 'I am not free ... I am not free.'

She accepted it, balanced it against some inner judgement and returned it to him. 'Yes, but now...?'

He could see that she loaded everything that held him, against the emotion that he roused in her, and that for her there were no alternatives. She was a child. She was not only a child but full of wisdom that could not be argued against. He came back and took her in his arms and kissed her again. 'Liv! Liv! I love you ... I do not want to talk about anything else ... now.' She said nothing, only pressed her cheek against his. It was enough for her. He heard a clock strike five somewhere from the streets outside them, and he remembered that he had asked a man to come to see him at five about a picture that he wanted to buy. He told her: 'I've got a man coming to buy a picture. Shall I let him in?'

'Why, of course, you must let him in!'

He laughed at her. That was another knight's move. 'What are you doing this evening?'

She had promised Mina Fuller to go there.

'I am going to the Fullers'. There is going to be some wonderful music. I promised Barbra to go with her. Mrs Fuller has found a boy — a hunchback, who plays some instrument marvellously.'

'I shall go, too.'

'Yes.' She caught her breath, making an assignation of it.

'I haven't been there since I met you.'

'No.' He seemed to make a reason of it. It confused her, giving her the mere surface of processes in him which she was unable to follow. She wanted to tell him that Barbra would not bring her to him, although she had asked her. And then she thought of Sasha and was silent. Nothing about him really mattered to her — except this — this was all that mattered. It made no difference when somebody rapped at the door, when an American came in and a deep, soft, drawling feminine voice said: 'Well, now, aren't you just too lovely for words!' mistaking her for a model. She smiled her good-bye to Per Malom and slipped away from them. She did not know what to do with herself, so she walked in the Luxembourg gardens, watched children turning out pailfuls of sand, and middle-aged women sewing, and mothers nursing their children, and old men looking like sacks flung on seats, exhausted, and quite ready to be emptied. They were outward and remote to her, as meaningless as the statues. The trees — the French trees — made dark spires in the air; graceful, and with a sort of reverie about them as though they had witnessed much in that garden. Everything, everything shone and moved for her like goldfish in a bowl of water, alive, yet confined. Within her there was no confinement....

She went to her hotel and changed her dress and then on to Barbra's studio, where she was to dine, in a sort of dream, upheld by the strong light within her. It was as though she dwelt in two worlds at once, a public and a secret one. Her eyes took in the outer world and conveyed its images to the inner one where it was blinded and diminished and deprived of its due importance. Her senses reflected the outer world and gave it nothing, whereas in secret there was no reflection. There was the truth itself, absorbing her into its elements.

Barbra was in an overall. She opened the door in a sort of rage, crying out to her as though she had been committing some crime: 'Where have you been? I went round to find you. I went twice, and you weren't there. Oh, Liv, I'm so unhappy. I've quarrelled with Sasha. I wanted to tell you, I wanted to tell somebody.'

'Quarrelled!' she repeated slowly, finding it an effort to comprehend that people could quarrel.

'Yes, yes. I suppose you think that that's nothing!'

'But no...' she answered gently. 'I think it is a great deal.' It truly seemed terrible to her, from the heights of her own harmony, that rupture could exist. 'You do ... care for him?' She put a doubt into speech.

Barbra was taking cold chicken and *macédoine des légumes* out of *charcuterie* cartons and putting them on thick Quimper plates. She jerked them out on the plates and said vehemently, without looking up: 'No! I don't care. I hate him, hate him ... I've never cared for anybody since Per Malom!'

The world within and the world without stood still for Liv. Her hands went cold. Her heart went ice-cold as she stood there listening to Barbra declaring her love for Per Malom. Sasha had said: 'Every new girl falls in love with him.' It took him away from her, divided him. And yet, deeper than these little facts, she had the knowledge that he was hers and indivisible, as she was his. It filled her with pity for Barbra, as though she had stolen him from her. She looked at her with a great sympathy in her eyes. Barbra, turning towards her, was caught in this look, washed in it, so that the rage went out of her, and her voice became natural again:

'It's all right Liv! Don't be sorry for me.'

Liv thought: it is best to say nothing. I can do nothing for her. It was not Per Malom's fault if everybody fell in love with him.

'Where were you? I went twice and each time you were out.'

She hesitated, then told the truth. 'I was at Per Malom's.'

'Liv! No! Did you go alone?'

'He took me there himself.'

Barbra stared, and was silent. When she spoke it was with fierce determination. 'He ought not to have taken you. I never wanted you to go. Yes, you may glare at me, Liv. I know what I am saying. You ought not to go.'

'Do you not think that I can take care of myself?' She had to defend herself, to refute the thoughts that were storming in Barbra's mind.

'Yes, yes! But can you take care of him?' Liv did not answer.

'I must tell you about him,' Barbra said.

She interrupted her: 'I do not want to hear anything about him.'

'Nonsense, Liv! You must know!'

'What can there be for you to tell me that I must know?' She wanted to put her hands over her ears, not to listen, to shut out every word. But she heard in spite of herself.

'That he is married, for instance....'

It froze through her, then thawed as she remembered that he had said: 'I am not free.' He had told her himself. Jacob Fuller had said that he was unhappy. She unfastened and refastened the catch of her belt, her head bent upon her fingers, shutting herself against every word.

'...that he makes love to every girl with any looks to speak of?'

'Sasha told me that ... I knew.'

'You knew! Oh, then, it's all right, if you know, if you don't care?'

'I don't care!' It was like shutting the gates in the wall of her defence, like shutting herself in with Per Malom into a state of siege.

'Well, then, if you don't care, then you won't mind knowing that he...' her voice quavered and steadied out again, 'he broke me in ... he was the first ... since then...'

She put her hands up then and pressed her face into them, pressing blindness into her eyes. She felt cold as death and without feeling. It was terrible to her to feel nothing, nothing but this coldness in which she and Per Malom had become as lifeless as statues. Deep down below the coldness there was one tiny prick of suffering (like the tiny prick that makes a mole bleed and brings it death) for Barbra. She was so sorry for Barbra, so sorry that she had quarrelled with Sasha, that she was unhappy....

'Oh, you see!'

It rang bells of mockery in her soul: 'You see!' She saw nothing. She felt nothing. She was so terribly sorry for Barbra. 'And Sasha?' she asked, her voice husky and strange, 'is it quite hopeless?'

'Quite. He has gone over to Josie Armstrong, Mina's friend. She feeds him better than I do. She has taken him to the tailor ... she has taken him to the tailor.'

'Taken him to the tailor?' It broke in upon her, thawing her into a torrent of real horror. 'Don't!' she cried out, swept at last completely into Barbra's power, defeated.

'You need not be so horrified. We all do it nowadays. The poor boys haven't the money. *Depuis la guerre! Depuis la guerre!* One has to be in the fashion. Besides, my dear girl, what difference does the money make — whether we give it and they take it, or they give it and we take it? A Frenchwoman wouldn't give it, of course. A Frenchman wouldn't take it, but we are not French ... we are Norwegian.'

Liv repeated it, twisting its meaning out of Barbra's meaning, making a flag of it: 'We are Norwegian!'

'No,' said Barbra, roused again, 'it isn't *because* we are Norwegian ... that has nothing to do with it. It is because we are *out* of our own country. We feel that we can do what we like and that people won't know, our own people, I mean. We never get to know the people of the country that we are in. We only know the foreigners, the people like ourselves ... we get out of our nationality, Liv, as we get out of our clothes.'

'Very much out of them!' she exclaimed bitterly. She did not mean to say anything bitter, for she was not feeling bitter. It escaped from her, making its own countermand against Barbra.

'Well, I shall never go back! I'm one of those who never go back!'

She thought instantly of Per Malom's mother, who had never gone back, and it became a sign of betrayal to her, of desertion. But she knew that Per Malom's mother paid for the desertion. She was there in Spain, in a land of fairest sunshine, where the flowers made her regret the flowers of her country. 'Oh!' she said in a low, deep note, 'it would be better to go back.'

'Why on earth did you come?' Barbra retorted upon her, '...to run away from Harald Christensen? You needn't marry him if you don't want to!'

'No,' she said, looking steadily in front of her and seeing for the first time the peacocks on Barbra's screen. The green-eyed tails spread out over the dark paint like flat lilies on a pond. 'I need not marry him ... if I don't want to.' The words were all on one note, dead, like a stone that has dropped to the bottom. The branches of the trees beyond the peacocks had dark spaces in between like yews in a churchyard. 'Today,' she added, 'I had a letter from my mother.'

'I had one, too,' said Barbra, and laughed. 'That was why I told you about Per Malom.'

Sympathy was torn from her like a cloak. There was nothing left. She stood, in some incomprehensible manner, naked before Barbra.

'It was, to say the least of it, a very direct letter. I know now what she thinks of me. Not much — does she?' She did not wait for Liv to answer. 'She wrote specially to say to me that if anything happened to you through your association with me that she would never forgive me! Behold me ... my brother's keeper! It's too funny! She made me frightfully angry. I was angry already, for I had just had it out with Sasha, so I was not in the sweetest of tempers. But, of course, she's right. You're much too good ... too good-looking to be let loose amongst us. She's quite right to look after her chicken!'

Liv felt humiliated, intensely humiliated, besieged with humiliation. She wanted to run away, to run away from them all and never see any of them again. Barbra's laughter was a flagellation. It whipped round her with a score of thongs. She was no longer frozen. Her blood was growing warm again, and going through her like pain.

Barbra, finished with laying the table, looked at her and was shot through with pity for her. It was as though the pity had passed out of Liv into her, where it was functioning for Liv as it had functioned in Liv for her. She quickened with remorse. She thought, seeing her as paintable: she is standing there like a gazelle. She had the hurt gentleness of a gazelle in her eyes. 'Poor child,' she murmured, and was cut short by Liv's passionate protest:

'Don't dare ... to pity me!' What was pity but the spill of rain hissing into the dry, burning desert, smarting? She would never be able to offer it again without remembering what it felt like. She walked away from Barbra, from Barbra's arms, to the other side of the table. 'This,' she said, raising the gazelle eyes, 'is what I suppose you would call — initiation!' There was a world of bitterness, of destruction, in her young voice. She would have given all that she possessed to be saying it to Aunt Sonja. Aunt Sonja was the only one who could have had the slightest conception of what it meant to her.

Barbra turned her back on her and was mute. She went behind the screen and emerged again with a dish of fruit. Her eyes were glistening. She put the fruit on the table, moving dishes to make room for it, arranging it carefully, over-carefully. Then, quickly, so that she had no warning, she went up to Liv and took her hands. 'Liv! Liv ... I am sorry ... I am so miserable!'

She wanted to free her hands and could not, so that she was forced to remain. She said clearly, wiping everything that was false out of her intention: 'But you know what you are going to do?'

Barbra dropped her hands, and went to her seat. 'What is there to do? I can do nothing.'

'Nothing about Sasha, except let him go....'

Barbra repeated it: 'Except let him go,' and began to serve Liv with the chicken. 'That,' she said, and felt very clever, 'is the pure policy of *laissez faire* ... of despair,' and got no answering cleverness from Liv.

Chapter Five

I t was very late when they arrived at the Fullers' studio. The stretch of long, illuminated windows shone like a lake of light in the darkness of the October night. The sky was clear and full of stars. Liv let Barbra go in in front of her, then slipped to the side and stood, regal as a queen, gazing into the crowd. The pride was terrible in her. It stretched and strained her so that she felt taller than she had ever felt in her life, and so full of sorrow that it felt like scorn upon her face. It seemed to her that it was impossible to look at any human being as an equal. She was above them and she was forced to look down upon them. They were so remote, so tiny, such queer little tortured figures, gyrating and chattering on the Fullers' floor. What did they mean? What did they mean to each other? Did they sting like bees? ... the one that mated the queen died of the act of love.... She shut her eyes. As certain as though she had seen him she knew that Per Malom was there and that he had found her. He would come to her. A sigh parted her lips. She moved into the throng, on a vague quest for Jacob Fuller. She wanted Jacob Fuller. Her intuition took her to him. He greeted her with both hands outstretched. 'My dear,' he said, 'I was afraid that you were not coming.' His speech was like mercy to her. 'They're all here tonight. The whole bunch ... even Sasha....' His eyes twinkled: 'You've heard....'

She cut him short. 'Yes. I know all about it.' So that was all they made of it. A joke. The latest scandal. Tomorrow they would be passing the interpretation along like a piece of money on the Dome terrace, and Chez les Vikings, all sorts of people would be able to read the expression on Barbra's face, to watch the blow scar and heal upon her.

'Hush!' he touched her arm. 'He's really good, this boy. Mina found him in a café in a back street.'

Mina Fuller's violinist had begun to play. The music came moaning in through the crowd, silencing it, transcending it. She took shelter in it, as in Jacob Fuller's presence. Per Malom was beside her. She kept her eyes wide, unflinching, wholly rapt in the distance, but she knew that he knew that she was aware of him. He will take me for an actress, she thought, a fine actress, pretending that there is nothing between us. It gave her courage somehow to believe that she was cheating him. No! He was being cheated by her appearance. She was hiding nothing except her wound.... The music truly had a power in it. She saw the violinist's face, sunk like a bas relief into the hunch of his shoulders. His eyes burned out upon them all and gave them nothing, nothing but that music that was like some wind encircling the world and raising the depths of the seas. She saw Mina Fuller resting in the storm in a periwinkle-blue frock, then the periwinkle-blue spot was whirled and lost to her, and the music took toll from all her senses. It took her from beginning to end with Per Malom and back again to the beginning, and there was no end ... no beginning. There was that between them which Time could not limit. She lost all her pride with him at her side, listening to that music, she lost her whole being to him.

She was saying to him: 'Take me! Take me!' in a million echoes of the music. And all the time she never once looked at him, never once stirred. She was as still as though she was frozen. The violinist's face was long, and peaked with strange endurance. His hands and face and feet were too big for the rest of him. His body had shrunk between his extremities, so that he ceased to be man and was a Trold with eyes and a brain. He could do what he liked with them, once they admitted his power. He was sending his music tearing through her, tearing her will to ribbons and filling her with a desperate wildness, with unbearable longing for Per Malom. A woman's profile leant out, rather gross, with full lips, holding a cigarette. It vanished, and she saw a long narrow strip of scarlet paint ending in a vase filled with haws. She and Mina Fuller had picked them in the woods of Meudon. They had picked them together long ago, ages ago. Only yesterday. The day before the day on which Per Malom had kissed her. The music went dark on her, taking her soul away from her and handing it to Per Malom. It was like anguish to stay so still, but she could not move. He was there beside her and she had not looked at him. He was watching her, reading her, knowing everything. Jacob Fuller said, slightly behind her: 'His name is Huniadi,' and Per Malom repeated it into her ear: 'His name is Huniadi.' Her '*Jah*' went back to him in a whisper. They were threaded together, speaking the violinist's name. 'It is Hungarian — that, that he is playing ... something of his own.' Something of his own! It was as foreign to her as his name — the fact that he could possess something that was his own. Something that you could neither eat, nor wear, nor destroy. She herself possessed nothing. She was utterly dispossessed, owning nothing. The music came to an end. That is to say, that the player's instrument dropped from his shoulder, and the power stopped in his hands, but the music went on and on as though it had entered her blood and would need much shedding. She turned quietly, knowing what she was doing, and looked at Per Malom with drained, exhausted eyes.

Jacob Fuller was there, so he said nothing, but his eyes gave her their own measure of his thoughts. There was about her tonight a dignity and richness that made him want to kneel to her. Her near presence stung him with a multitude of arrows, so that he asked himself: 'God! God! Am I falling in love?' And Tana's image was blown into scattered petals in a storm. His life became a waste behind her, and he felt that only through her could it become fertile again, mean anything. She made him feel that everything had been spoiled for him, and that he was standing amidst ruins and desiring her. She would take him away with her into some place where there was no destruction. There was an eternal youth about her, a spirit in which nothing would wilt nor perish. He wanted to be alone with her. She made all the other women in the room seem trivial, decorated, aided by their clothes.

'He has been in prison...' said Jacob Fuller's husky voice. 'Forgery, I think. You must ask Mina. He has confessed his sins to her. Look at his hands ... he has those sort of hands.'

She looked at his hands. Large hands with a strange delicacy about them, the hands of a being who asked more of life than it could ever give him.

'A mistake! Surely a grave mistake,' said Per Malom.

She looked at him, caught by the note of sympathy. A change had taken place in him. It opened him to her, made her more vulnerable than ever. She stayed close to Jacob Fuller.

'The hands of a strangler, I should say; hunchback's hands....'

'Don't! ... that is brutal!' she cried.

Jacob Fuller smiled at her, and she saw the butcher's shop behind him and a knowledge of physical things that was both true and horrible. 'I never see a hunchback without having that ... that feeling that they could strangle....'

'They have not the strength, those long fingers,' Per Malom went further, and killed the truth with truth.

She was grateful to him. It made her say: 'It is, perhaps, in them, in themselves, that something has been strangled, stifled.'

'Yes,' he said, 'it is in them,' and, looking deeply at her, he added: 'It is in all of us ... something stifled.'

She sighed, keeping the sigh secret, and said nothing. Suddenly Jacob Fuller went away from her side, and she was alone with Per Malom. All about them were many people, gay, chattering people. But they were alone.

'Liv!'

She looked at him for answer.

'Will you slip away presently, come to my studio, where we can talk?'

Quite close to them a girl in a dark-red velvet dress, with beautiful white shoulders, was sitting and looking up at a man with a coquettish expression. She was like a flower enticing some insect. The man meant nothing to her beyond something that she wanted from him, something momentarily possible, like admiration.

'Come!' he repeated, and made a way for her through the groups of people. He did not see her hesitation, nor see it change in her, as though it had been cowardice, into courage.

She said to herself, following him: 'I am coming with you. I am coming with you. I am coming with you to the end of the world.' For it would be the end — to her. They went out into the street, under the clear October stars. The dark air had the clarity that comes before rain. They walked in silence. At the corner, when they turned round to go into his street, he slipped his arm through hers. He opened the door for her, as he had opened it only a few hours ago. Everything was a repetition. It was being repeated for her as though there was some fear that she might be able to forget it. She could have found her way to the window in the darkness, but nevertheless she waited while he switched on the light. It came with such a glare that she almost cried out for it to be dark again. But to ask for the darkness with him made her flush with shame. She accepted the glare, and following the lesson that had been set, went to the window. It seemed to her that it would take all their lives for them to say all that had to be said to each other. Yet there was no haste, no need to hurry, no need to chase in haste, one fragment of it.

He came down to her and took her into his arms. 'Liv! What is it about you? What is it? Why did you not come before this?'

'Why? Why?' She yielded in his arms, and her own arms went about him. She lifted her face to his. She needed no wooing. 'I love you,' she said.

Her face was beautiful between the darkness against the window and the bright silver glare of the room. She healed him, made him whole.

'I love you ... and it is too late.'

He held her close, tenderly, passionately, denying by their contact that it could be too late. But he knew it was true. It was a whole lifetime too late. 'No...' he murmured.

He kissed her and she drew herself out of his arms and went to a deep chair. She sat down on the arm of the chair, and turned towards him with a movement that gave him her face in three-quarters, with the chin curving down into her long, firm throat. 'Tell me!' she waited.

He took in her beauty, worshipping her, and at the same time feeling her there as his equal, the woman who was meant to march side by side with him. She lifted them both to a plane where there was no equivocation, where, drained from the utmost of facts of living, they were real and themselves. It lengthened out for him as upon a long voyage, the rapture that she roused in him, the strength that was as though she said (she sat there and said nothing) everything that has been said and done was meant for this. This is the whole meaning. He realised, before her, that there is one love that drowns all the others. There is one love in which all others melt as in an image. She took the charm of every other woman away from him. And the miracle was that she did not parch him, as Tana had done. She filled him with the triumph of a man who has passed his dangers. She took his youth and broke it, made a shell of it, so that he stood out, clear and strong, and was himself with her. 'There is much ... to tell.'

'I know.'

'If you know,' he said gently, reaching down to her sources, 'why need I tell you?'

Her eyes and mouth were sorrowful. 'Tell me.'

He came and sat in the chair below her. 'I will try to tell you....' He clasped his hands under his chin and looked up at her, 'There is much to tell.'

She spread her hand on the back of the chair behind him and closed it again, feeling acutely the soft silken rib of the material.

'I am married.'

She knew that, so she waited. She was indifferent. His marriage meant no more to her than the beards that had been shaven from him, that she had never seen. What had been taken from him made him no less hers.

He let the silence reach its last gasp, and then he said: 'It was a very unhappy marriage, one of those marriages that are made in the cradle.'

'That,' she said, thinking of Harald Christensen, 'is no reason why it should be disastrous.'

'You are right. It did not go wrong because of that.... It was, all the same, that sort of marriage. We were married because there was no hedge between our fields. She was a half-wit. She is now in an asylum.'

'Was ... was there no way out of it?'

'None! She comes of an episcopal family ... and in Spain! No, there is no way out.' He added in another second: 'What do you expect?'

'Nothing, except that, of course, you fell in love with another woman!' Other women had fallen in love with him. He had the quality that made it inevitable. She was one in a procession.

She knew that she was but one and at the same time it made no difference to her, for she knew that she meant more. She measured him by her own values and brought him up to them.

'I was twenty-three, married, and with no wife. She went crazy when there was a child coming.... I met a girl. A girl of my own class. In Spain, you know, we have very rigid notions. She was the loveliest creature ... you saw her portrait.' She said nothing, so he went on: 'We loved each other ... we had each other ... it lasted three years.' As the words left his mouth they seemed to contract for him, to close up into a tiny mirror in which their scope was lessened. Tana went into the distance and stood, a perfect image, unforgettable, on the rim of days that belonged almost to his childhood. Far away, filmy and intangible as first love. 'I have never been able to forget her, never for one moment....'

'That I quite understand.' How could it be otherwise?

'Until now ... until you.'

She accepted it as the bare truth and was unmoved, unflattered, by it. It lessened nothing of her suffering.

'What is it, Liv, that you have done to me?' He turned round to her, asking her with all his force to show him where she was taking him.

'I ... I have done nothing. Isn't it, Per, what has been done to us?' She had to make him see that it had been done to her, too. It came clear to her as to a saint ready for sacrifice. 'You see, I ... I knew nothing of what love was like ... until that first day that I saw you. It came ... it is quite terrible.' She linked her hands together on her knee.

He regarded her bowed head, the young droop of her body, and was agitated by her, by the tragic lowness of her voice, into a great tenderness. He longed to protect her, to shelter her, to enfold her in his strength, where nothing could have any power to hurt her. He put his arm round her and tried to draw her down into the chair, into his arms.

This time she resisted him. She darted from him, and stood, linking and relinking her hands, at a little distance, and repeated to him: 'It is terrible!'

He stood up and held out his arms to her. He desired miserably to break her terror, to show her the other side — the exaltation, and at the same time he felt that he could teach her nothing. Her exaltations were far greater than his. It was she who was the giver. She had gifts that he never possessed, and could only possess through her....

She did not move. 'Tell me,' she said, making a shield of the question, 'about all the others ... and why....'

His hands dropped, and he rammed them into his pockets. 'And why?' He shrugged his shoulders. 'Are they worth it? There were so many!'

'Why?'

She probed for the motive. She had a Day of Judgment air, a very young Day of Judgment, standing there and asking so simply for his reasons. He had a spasm of resentment. He was urged swiftly to defy this side of her, to treat her ... as he might have treated any other girl. It made him say curtly, as though the fact that she had resisted his arms gave him a right to take that tack with her. 'Why should I tell you? It doesn't matter. It doesn't matter to us.'

'If you were unhappy,' she said simply, 'I could understand.' She was thinking of Barbra, resenting that he had made her friend suffer, made a play of this state of feeling which was so great that nobody in their proper senses could play with it.

She plunged him into her sympathy. There was neither guilt nor blame before her. It was as though he were standing face to face with himself, comprehending himself in her presence. 'Yes. I was very unhappy. I was wretchedly unhappy. After Tana went ... there was no need for her to have gone. She still loved me. She loves me still. I love her too, Liv, and always will....'

'I know. You cannot kill love.'

'She suddenly got frightened when her husband began to run after other women. She went back to her husband. She was frightened. It made her cruel ... cruel to me. She laughed at me. It was that, Liv, that she could deny me and laugh at me. It raised a thousand devils in me. I didn't care what I did. I took every woman who came. I revenged myself on them. You can...' he added, in a pause when she said nothing, 'make a habit of it. Then I had a whole year when I kept clear of women. I went into the desert. I began to paint. I've been everywhere in Central Europe ... trying to forget her. I came back...' he made a gesture of impotence, '... there is my painting, of course. It means a great deal to me.'

She said, 'Yes, you have that!'

He strode away with his back to her, to the window, where he turned and said down the space of the room to her: 'I've made a wreck of everything — marriage, love ... my life!'

They exchanged a long searching look. She was silent, and he turned from her again and stared into the darkness. She had stripped him of everything. He had made a wreck of his life. He was not free, and he had attained nothing. He had money, as much as he wanted, and it did not save him from wreckage. She was there and he loved her, loved her with a love that made him bankrupt.... He went down to the edge of unbelief where all is ashes. Far away beyond the tree he saw the contours of streets marked by lights like stars, the streets of Paris that look like hills in the distance, poetic, winding as the first lanes must have wound when men began to tramp them. In the dim night they had this magic. He was warmed from despair, looking at them, feeling their beauty. He returned to that realm of male consciousness where power springs from the gift to mould plastic earth, build cities and bridges, and make transports scream with burdens, to take stones and shape them. He felt that because he had met her he would be able to see things differently, put a new passion into his work. They would share ... he would build....

'Per!'

He moved round and she was there at his side. He had not heard her. This time it was she who was holding out her arms. He gathered her into his, her voice breaking against his ears:

'I cannot bear to hear you talk like that! Oh, my dear, my dear, I cannot, cannot bear to hear you talk so bitter!'

'It is not bitterness!' he soothed her, all the bitterness gone out of him. 'It's a sort of reckoning.' Her face drooped back from him. He took his fill of her wonder, the tragic sweetness, the youth, all that she offered him. 'Now that you have come....' He felt a current run through her in his arms, '...now that you have come....'

She was torn with desire to cry out to him: 'Yes, yes, I have come. I am here. Take me. I will make everything different.' She took his face between her hands and pulled it down to her, examining him with steadfast eyes. 'Yes, it is true....'

'Then what else matters?'

It wasn't that nothing else mattered, but that this mattered more than anything. Her body and soul depended upon it. She was racked by decision. He would never be free. He was not free. And immediately she thought of his freedom she went back upon the thought in mockery. Free or not free, he was hers. They were each other's. She could make no terms with the miracle. She was filled with a magnificent patience. She felt like one of those women, far back in her race, seeing her Viking go forth on his journey, leaving her to face the absence and the loss. She said:

'We shall always belong to each other.'

He was conscious of the condition behind her avowal. It trembled behind the strength in her eyes. He knew that she was capable of breaking her life to pieces for his sake. She was young enough for anything. He felt suddenly so much older, so burdened with experiences of women that deprived him of the right to take her. Had she come in Tana's hour and place he would not have hesitated. He was older now, he had suffered, he knew what the world could do. Ah! It was none of those things. It was simply that he did not feel worth her, worth the sacrifice that she would have to make. And then he was swept from all these considerations on to her own plane. It was, as his mother had said: 'In the North we love with our souls!' He loved her with an intensity that would outlast her presence. Whether she was there or not, this love for her would never die in him. They could not be separated.

He could not desecrate a love like that. His arms dropped from her. He walked away and came back, standing a little from her. 'Tell me,' he said quietly, 'about you ... about your life?'

'There is nothing to tell.' She smiled at him with strange sweetness, 'I have just lived, been a child, and grown up ... always at home....'

'Nothing else?' He was smiling, too, wanting to hear the minutest things about her.

'There's Harald Christensen ... and Aunt Sonja.'

'Tell me about them.'

'Harald? Well now, that is another affair that began in the cradle. They all want me to marry him. He has wanted it for a long time.' She said it casually, as the mere statement of something that was true, but underneath the casualness she was conscious for the first time of what her denial meant to Harald Christensen. She suffered for him a pang of pity, knowing now what love meant.

The possibility of her marriage with this vague Harald Christensen flashed through Per's consciousness, and he imagined her bearing ghostly children. They were ghostly, in this instant to him, but to her they would be tangible and all too solid, and it was he who would be her ghost. It was he who would be vague and shadowy to her, the ghost from this youth which she possessed at present, but which would be smothered in her maturer years by strange activities. And instantly he contradicted the assumption of these things and knew that whether she married or not he had entered into her life to remain. She would never forget him. But when he tried to realise her as the wife of another man he felt that he could not and would not let her go. He had the power to keep her....

'Then there's Aunt Sonja! I would like you to know Aunt Sonja.'

She had the air of sharing a great treasure with him. He asked: 'She is very wonderful?'

'She is very wonderful,' she repeated, and left him, in spirit, for Aunt Sonja. Aunt Sonja, stooping to touch Olaf's head with her lips, walking like a queen through those queer, shabby rooms of her house in the Rindalsholm. And there, gathered up for her, against the walls of the present, the full meaning of Aunt Sonja's message. Aunt Sonja had known ... this. Clearly, as if it had been written out for her on a piece of paper, she knew that Aunt Sonja had loved like this, loved and given herself to the man she loved. It accounted for that strange sorrow that came into her face when she was tranquil, that lay like a shadow beyond the light of all her expressions, and hid itself in every touch and act. She looked at Per Malom, loving him to the roots of her being, yet seeing him through her aunt's experience, seeing what had been done to Aunt Sonja. It became unbearable to her that anything should be broken between her and Per Malom.

'You will tell her about this ... about me?'

She answered: 'Yes. I will tell her.'

He looked at her long and deeply. 'That means, Liv, that there will be nothing to tell.'

She bowed her head to shut out his expression, and then she looked up and cried to him: 'What is the use?'

'The use...!' He shrugged his shoulders. He wouldn't have called it use. She did not mean use in the sense of utility. She meant the completest futility. And she was right. He experienced an extraordinary fatigue about it. Hope was rubbed out of his senses. With this Aunt Sonja behind her he was impotent. It was as though she had taken an ally. 'Yes,' he said dully, 'you'd better go.'

When he said it like that he made of it a desertion so flagrant that she could not go. She went to him, caressing him with her hands. 'Not like that, Per, not like that.'

Her touch maddened him, made him brutal. He gave her no answering caress. 'Like that or not like that, what does it matter? If you go, you go. You must go! You are a young girl. You don't know what you are doing. Go, Liv! I'm not worth you. I've told you that I've spoiled my life. There is no reason why I should spoil yours.'

'You couldn't!' She shook her head at him, her eyes lit and gentle. 'And it isn't true that I do not know what I am doing. I know quite well. I knew when you asked me to come up here with you what I was going to do. You see...' she pressed her fingers into his sleeve as though to press the poison of the sting out of her words, 'Barbra told me all about you. She told me this afternoon. I knew ... I knew ... that it was hopeless....'

'Yet you came up here with me?'

'To say good-bye....'

'To say good-bye,' he mocked, staring at her as though she had played him false.

She swept falseness out of it. 'And to tell you, Per, how I love you, how I love you for ever and ever. Nothing matters except that I love you ... and that it is too late. I feel,' she added, after a tiny pause, in which the accusation died out of his eyes and he kissed her, 'that I have lived through a whole lifetime here in this place with you....'

Her deep contralto voice was full of dreaminess, pouring through him in a healing stream. She recovered for him his first belief in women. 'Go on,' he whispered.

'Somewhere, ages ago, we belonged to each other ... it is a memory. Or is it that it is yet to come? I don't know. You've had so many women, Per, you know what it is.... You don't want me like that?'

He held her as if he could never let her go. 'No, no! You are different from any of them.'

There was a silence, then she said: 'Then it isn't good-bye! Good-bye is a stupid word. There is no good-bye between us.'

'No.' He wanted her to stay for ever in his arms. 'When I saw you first I said — she is the sort that gives all or nothing!'

'Don't be unhappy!' she smiled, teasing the gloom out of him. 'Which have I given you ... nothing?'

'Everything!' he cried, and renounced her.

After a little she said, putting her arm through his and turning him round: 'Come, we will make a little voyage together. You will show me your pictures, your things, the things you live with ... so that I shall remember them.'

It was only when she said that, that he really felt that he had lost her. But as he went round the room with her, showing her trivial things and watching her touch them — like the little flat travelling clock which she pressed between her hands, feeling the morocco case against her cheek — he had the sense of storing up her manner, her touch, her voice, her laughter, so that for him, too, these trifles would always have power to evoke her image, and she would, instead of being lost, always be there.

'I have a little clock like that, only mine is blue and it is scratched. It was scratched by a kitten. We always seem to have a kitten. My sister Astrid loves them. Yes, there is always a kitten in our house.'

What a child she was! Telling him as though it was the most wonderful thing in the world, that there was always a kitten in the house.

In telling him she felt that she was putting her childhood far, far away. She could see it so plainly because of the distance. He was there before her, so real and close and terrible that nothing about him was plain to her. She would have to escape from him in order to be able to understand, and it was not true at all that she knew what she was doing. She did not know. She did not know what to do with herself before him. In a moment she was lost. It made her dart to the door, then turn and pause, the pause beating in her like a drum. And yet, in the same moment that filled her with such fear, she felt as she had felt in the Fullers' doorway, when she had not dared to search for him, tall and strained with such pride and anguish as needed only a little thing to turn it into bliss. She saw the stretch of Algerian curtain, the painting of the Dolomites sculptured, it seemed, out of sunlight as though he had painted it from some blaze in his spirit; she saw the portrait of Tana turned against the wall and thought — he will never make me into a portrait, a portrait that you can turn against a wall. 'I must go,' she said and did not even put out a hand.

He reached her and crushed her into his arms: 'Don't go....'

The bliss and anguish ran together, and then the anguish raced out and the bliss perished. 'Don't...' She pressed closer to him, 'ask me to stay! Don't, Per! ... be fair!' It was a cry to save them both, to save her from the hurt that she was going to inflict upon him.

He buried his head in her breast, and she held it there, looking out over him with a woman's grief in her eyes. Presently she put her hands on his shoulders and pushed him away. Her voice was steady and very clear, saving each of them from mistake. 'Stay here. Let me go alone.'

She opened the door herself and went out and shut it after her, and went down the long corridor towards the end where the street-light burned and beckoned her from peril. Any moment he could have come after her, caught her up, but she knew (as if the preservation came from within herself) that he would not follow her. 'There!' she thought, 'that is all for tonight.' It was not ended. It had only begun. It would never end.

And Per, in the room that she had left, was thinking the same thing — that it had begun.

With the night air blowing in her face Liv went up the street, feeling as though she had been through war with him and come out victorious, but in rags and tatters, and so tired. She was so tired that she wanted to cry, to sit on a door-step and cry on his shoulder.

She found Barbra on the Fullers' door-step, smoking a cigarette.

'Behold me!' cried Barbra, 'the last of the Mohicans. The captains and the kings have gone — meaning Sasha. You have no idea how late it is. I was making ready to set out to rescue you. Look! I've got your shawl!' She held it up and shook it into a ghost's shape before Liv's eyes.

'But you didn't...' Liv began.

'Yes, I did. I knew where you were. Everybody knows.'

'*Quelle publicité!*' she said sharply, roused and angry. But she melted immediately before the poise of Barbra's figure, the ghost-shawl lying limp in her arms. 'Well, it doesn't matter!' She was too tired to fish implications from their depths.

'I never said it did.' Barbra's voice was acrid. 'Nothing on this earth matters. Here, take your shawl and put it on, it's quite chilly at this hour of the morning, and come down with me to the Vikings.'

'Isn't it too late?'

Barbra laughed at her. 'My dear girl! Is it ever too late? And the rest, and the early bird catches the worm. I feel as though it would drive me crazy to go to bed.'

She remembered Sasha. Barbra was making a flaunt of her misery. 'Don't go, Barbra. Don't go there, where everybody knows you. Listen, I'll go anywhere else with you, anywhere where there aren't people who know you. Let us go for a walk?'

'I've danced so much that I'm not able to cross the street, let alone walk to the next bistro. I'm waiting for a taxi. That is what I am really doing — waiting for a taxi, for somebody to come home in this forsaken street.'

Presently a taxi really did come and stopped and a man got out of it. Barbra called to the chauffeur and gave him the direction. 'You can,' she said, seeing the man consider if she knew what she was asking him to do — to take her a distance that could be walked in three minutes, 'take us as far as the Place Vendôme, and bring us from there to the Vikings.' She got in beside Liv. 'He thinks, as you did, that I am quite drunk.' Liv was silent. In a moment she spoke again. 'What do you think? Sasha was there!' She heard Liv's protest and paid no attention to it. 'It was Mina's fault. Josie Armstrong's her friend; she shouldn't have let her come or she should have sent them away early.'

Liv put her hand on her knee. Her voice was warm with sympathy. 'You shouldn't have stayed.'

She pushed the hand roughly away. 'Behaved like a fool, you mean. Run away, as though I'd done something disgraceful. *They* ought to have had the grace to go. They were,' she laughed mirthlessly, 'the victors. Mina ought to have sent them.'

'They ought to have gone, but when they didn't, it would have been better, Barbra, not to have stayed, not to let them see....'

'I let them see nothing. I was neither sad nor gay — no extremes. I was perfectly normal ... quite hard....'

That was it, Liv thought, the hardness. It concealed nothing. 'I wish you hadn't stayed,' she repeated stupidly.

'It would have spoiled the fun, my dear. Everybody was intensely amused. It was as good as a play. As Olga Wienawski says, nobody will go to a concert to hear good playing, only a few half-wits who happen to love music, but if you could promise that the pianist would take poison beforehand, and die in writhing agony on the keyboard, the box-office would be stormed. Boxing-matches, bull-fights, and human torture ...

that is the breath of life to them! Oh, my dear, I am only doing my share to save them from monotony!'

They arrived at the Vikings with that phrase: 'To save them from monotony' ringing in their ears. In the upward glow from the windows the ship shone clear. It hung there as a symbol of adventuring. It had travelled a long way to become this symbol of adventuring. It seemed to Liv that the old sea-kings were dead, and that, even as their ships had been stolen out of the earth, something had been robbed from them. The ship hung there as the symbol of a recklessness that was never theirs, yet which had, in some intricate manner, been taken from them. A recklessness that would never be crowned in Trondjem. Here was no Olav's well of purification. Here, she felt, looking over Barbra's shoulder, and seeing the fair faces of Norwegian women, hearing the soft Norwegian voices, is the same spending of the body — women's beauty and men's strength. They were wasting it with that lavishness that marked her race. And for what? To win no seas, to make no heroes. It was, as Barbra said, to save them from monotony. The world came down to that.

Barbra greeted friends. The Wilses were there, a girl whose name was Gudrun, and two dark boys in the uniform of the French Air Force. Barbra did not stay with them, she passed to a table in the inner room, in an alcove where there were two vacant seats. She hung up her coat and sat down, and propped her elbows on the table. 'Talk to me, Liv! Tell me, you are so closed up! Tell me about Per! Did he make wonderful love to you? He can!'

Liv was thankful that her head came above Barbra's, so that she could hide her expression. She was dumb. She felt as helpless as an animal on a surgeon's table about to be cut open to see how it worked. The waiter came and saved her for a moment. She chose coffee. She would not be able to sleep afterwards. But whether she took coffee or not she would not be able to sleep. She saw the flowers hanging in brackets like the flowers on a ship, and she wished that she was truly on a ship going away from all this. She had come here for Barbra's sake, to be with her, to save her as far as she could about the Sasha affair, but if Barbra was going to drag her own torment into it, she would get up and run away, run into the street, run anywhere, run back to Per Malom....

'I don't have much luck,' said Barbra bitterly, 'with my men.'

'You should wait,' she said in a leap from her thoughts, 'until they run after you!' She was sorry that she had said it. She had thought it and was so afraid that Barbra would jump again to Per Malom that she jumped herself, and said something that was stupid.

'The holy virgin idea! Oh, my dear girl! I am a little beyond that. I'm not beautiful, you know. I'm not attractive to men!'

'You have your painting!'

'Do you really think that anything makes up to a woman for love?'

'No,' she answered slowly, 'I did not mean that.' She thought of her aunt. 'I mean that one can put love into ... into what one does.'

'They also serve who only stand and wait!'

'Well, don't they?'

'They are saints! I belong to the sinners!'

Chapter Five

At the table in front of them a Dutch sailor was pointing out to his companion a route on a map that he had spread out. She heard the names Bergen and Lubeck, and saw the boats going through the Hjelte and Fedje fjords, and had a sudden heartache. It was so hot and close in here, and such a lot of chatter, such a lot of men and women, and Barbra trying to be hard. What did it all mean? And Per Malom standing in the studio, where she had been in his arms. In leaving him she felt that she had left herself — the self that she had been and would never be again. Aunt Sonja came back into her mind. Aunt Sonja, who was so very, very far away from all this. She wondered what Aunt Sonja would think of this place — this place that was like a ship and was no ship, just as the men in it were no Vikings. A Norwegian had flown across the Atlantic and had come here and inscribed his name on a carafe. He had brought the breath of the Vikings into it. They were the new Vikings — the men who sailed the air. And what they found here, in this rendezvous at the end of the journey, was no worse nor no better than it had ever been. Always there were women leaning over a table to greet the men who returned....

A big broad-shouldered young man came towards them. Barbra whispered in her ear, pretending to search for something in the pocket of her coat: 'Here's Bernt Strom. He knows about Sasha.'

He greeted them, found a stool, and squashed his large form in at their table. 'How goes it?' he gave Barbra a subtle knowing smile.

She returned it, crinkling her long lashes together. 'We two,' she said, nodding at Liv, 'are a perfect representation of that apparatus that is found in railway carriages. You turn it to the right...' she spread out her right hand, 'and then to the left ... It is marked "On" and "Off" ... hot and cold ... I am left!'

They laughed together, and their laughter ran through Liv's veins horribly, like an impure thing. In front of them, at the table beyond the Dutch officer, a middle-aged woman was clutching the coat of a man who was going away with a young, pretty girl; she was pleading with her eyes, with the eyes of a dumb beast, to the man not to go, and he was visibly moved by her pleading, pitying her, and yet resolved behind the pity to go with the girl. You could see all the love in the older woman rising and endowing her with the last remnants of her beauty, as autumn strains its colours through dying leaves. Afterwards she would perish in the first wind that came. There would be no more beauty, only the beauty that was secret and within her, hidden under the white head of winter. Liv could not help seeing. She was stormed with remorse for the woman, seized, as when one meets a funeral in the street, by that regret which, knowing nothing of the dead, yet misses them and feels the void where they have been.

Bernt Strom was speaking to her. 'You are lucky. You are not out in the cold, shivering!'

She stared at him as though he were speaking a language that she did not understand. She was not out in the cold — shivering! Oh, fool! Fool! What was he talking about? And then, guarding herself into a pretence that would save her from argument, from unbearable protests, she controlled her expression and smiled back at him, and said: 'Poor Barbra!'

as though it was of Barbra that he had been speaking. It directed him upon Barbra.

'Lots of other fish in the sea!'

'Lots of other fish in the sea,' Barbra chanted.

'There's me, for instance!' He leaned across to her, his massive body in its loose mauve-grey tweed looking rather like a monstrous jellyfish.

'There's you ... and lots of others, lots of other fish in the sea!' She smote him down with his own weapon, and laughed at him, hard laughter, that had a triumph in it.

'Poor Barbra!' He repeated Liv's phrase like an automaton.

'I feel,' said Barbra, 'that I would like to get drunk, really drunk, so that you,' she looked at Liv as though she knew quite well that she was tormenting her, 'would have to carry me home.' She saw the horror rise and drown again in Liv's eyes, and went on, 'but not here! That would be giving them too much for their money!' She looked round at the crowded tables. 'Isn't it odd, one can never get drunk in private, alone, I mean? It can only, it appears, be accomplished in a crowd. A sort of ... the bread and the circus all together!'

'Men can!' he said, regarding her stupidly, as though her wits were too sharp to keep up with.

'Ah men! They are a race apart. They are not like us, they are so self-sufficient! Don't you agree, Liv?'

Liv sipped her coffee, which was nearly cold. 'Are they?' she asked, and passed the problem on to the heavy Bernt Strom.

'I've been reading Keyserling,' said that young man, and launched into an analysis which amazed her, not for the worth of what he was saying, but because it revealed to her how the male intellect could function in the oddest places and maintain its rationality in circumstances where a woman's reason would only hold together by the grace of God and her instincts. It brought her the oddest relief. It had a sort of mercy about it — like clothes. She did not listen to him. She could not make herself interested, but she took cover under the shower of his opinions and was alone with her own thoughts. Alone with her hunger for Per Malom. He was still standing where she had left him. In her mind he was still standing there, and his eyes had that dark pain in them that she wanted to appease. She was bewildered, wondering what was the real thing to do, the thing that would ring true at the end of everything. Honestly she did not know. She had gone away from him. But where had she gone to? Where was she going to? Tomorrow he would find her ... and the next day, and this hunger for him would grow and grow until she could endure starvation no longer.... Bernt Strom was saying: 'Austrian men are male and Englishmen female,' and the Dutch boy was folding up his map. The names Bergen and Stettin, Lubeck, seemed to rise in the cigarette fumes like sky-writing — the letters jumbled and standing on their corners. Bergen! Bergen! The word grew and swelled in her senses, and quite suddenly as though it had, like the word in the sky, taken quick sense from the jumble, she knew that it was written out for her, that it had a meaning. It was like the words that St Augustine had heard in the garden turning him against the Manicheans. It was calling her. And beyond it she saw the outstretched arms of Aunt Sonja, the silence, the blessed silence of Stortoppen, and the long dark Northern winter, in which she could hide and be made strong again....

Abruptly, without a word of explanation to Barbra she rose and went over to the Dutchman, catching him before he went away.

'Excuse me,' she said, speaking quickly, 'but can you tell me ... I could not help overhearing you say that you are going to Bergen ... can you tell me when there is a boat? I want to go back, I have to go to Norway immediately!'

He looked up, his eyes gave her swift praise, he half rose from his seat, was embarrassed by the woman next him, and sat down again, and, putting his hand into his breast pocket brought out a sheaf of printed leaflets. 'If you must go immediately, there's ... you must catch the German train, which goes early tomorrow, I mean this morning, in a few hours.'

She took the leaflets that he gave her, thanked him, and went back to Barbra. They were both watching her, a sleek, hazy amusement in their expressions.

'My, you are coming on!' Barbra purred.

'I am going home,' she said curtly.

'You can go,' Barbra retorted, thinking that she meant that she was going home to her hotel, 'Bernt Strom will take care of me.'

'Come with me,' she pleaded, confused in her own mind as to whether she meant, like Barbra, to the hotel, or as she meant herself, to Norway.

Barbra looked up at her, looked at the lovely face that was shining down upon her in such sad seriousness. Inexplicably she loved her in that moment, as women love women who give them trust. She put out her hand and touched Liv's sleeve. 'My child ... I cannot....'

She saw Barbra's will falter and wave, very white and far, like a flag on an outpost. Little muffled figures flew past her in a snowstorm from some scene in her childhood, turned the corner, and vanished. 'Come!' she said again, and waited.

'Come where, what do you mean? Liv!'

'I'm going ... I'm going back to Norway....'

Barbra laughed, and Bernt Strom laughed, unholy unbelieving laughter, Judas laughter that rattled like thirty pieces of silver. 'Well go, my child, go! I'll come round for breakfast!'

She went out from them, feeling as though she had been sold. Out into the street where the ship still shone, as in a shrine, above the lights. Overhead the day pushed a thin streak of dawn through the stars.

Chapter Six

It was Olaf's birthday. Sonja Krag was preparing his breakfast-tray on a table by the window. She had come down early to do it before he was awake. There was the large flat cake — as large as the face of a church-clock when you see it from the ground — with his name on it and two skis crossed in angelica on the white icing. There were the new fret-work stencils he had asked for, the knife with seven blades and a camera from his father, and from her the translation of Hans Andersen and the sports suit that she had been knitting for weeks, never letting him see her working at it. She had begun it before Pastor Evensen's funeral. She stood by the window fingering the bright blue garments, stretching mechanically the white Xs of the pattern, thinking: 'Another birthday!' The others were big boys now. He would soon be like them. They would grow so strong that they would have no need for her and they would turn from her into that comradeship for which their father waited. It was all nonsense, what was said about sons belonging to the mothers and daughters to the fathers. They reached a destroying age when they wanted neither father nor mother, and by the time you recaptured them it was almost time to leave them. Nothing could be done about it. One could only be careful not to waste a moment of their possessions. Olaf was hers now. He would go, like the others. He would be like Liv Evensen, the Viking strain would cry out in him and he would go over the sea. He would return. They all returned — to the mystery and magic of their land. The ones who stayed away were those who had escaped the magic....

Trangfoss fell steadily in the distance, and the twilight sky was grey and tranquil, with silver clouds patterned on the tranquillity as the wind on sand. The wood stove crackled occasionally, and the room was full of pleasant warmth. She had not turned on the electric light. She liked the twilight of these mornings, the closing breath of the winter days. She could never explain it even to herself, but it was as a ritual to her when the leaves dropped off the trees, and the branches made bare arches in the forest, and the snows thickened; the crown of Stortoppen grew and glistened and poured over her nose and right down over the Rindalsholm. She loved the purity of the snow, the whiteness, as of an altar-cloth, that went over the earth. She sang a little song, standing there, a folk-song that went with the firelight in it — '*Heil du fare, heil du heim komme.*' She felt very happy, waiting to draw the curtains and turn on the light for Olaf's birthday breakfast.

On a morning like this morning, years ago, she had passed through the Dovrefjeld mountains, feeling that her heart was as cold as the winter and would never warm again. She remembered perfectly the drive, the coming out of the forest towards her home, her mother's unsmiling greeting, and Anna saying: 'Well, you have come back!' And then her mother's: 'Sonja, you ought to have written to tell us that you were coming.' She had answered, hiding a world behind her, that she was sorry that she had not written. Her mother was distressed because no proper welcome had been prepared for her in the home. She had returned like a fugitive, they said. And it was true; a fugitive flying from truth, from a reality that had become horrible, into the perishing snows, where the true and the false are crystallised out into the beauty of dreams. The mountains had greeted her. She had gone through the dark-walled fjords into a dark peace of soul. She was already better when she arrived, able to stand quiet without wringing her hands and to answer with ordinary sense when people spoke to her. The Dovrefjeld had been wonderful to her, saying: 'See, and see!' And, opening beauty after beauty as one takes jewels out of a box. She had had to accept the beauty, to take it with cold hands, and take it to her heart, which was too cold for love, and she had, even then, piercing her own chilled senses, argued that the beauty of the Dovrefjeld was only the beauty of the end of the world.... Her own world had come to an end.

It was in Trondjem that she had met her husband. He had come down from Sulitelma to find a wife, and he had found her.... He needed her. He said he loved her. And to be needed was the utmost stretch of human mercy....

Trangfoss had already begun to change its note, to hum the winter from its source, the winter which closed and hushed everything, and drew Life into the darkness, folding its treasures in white and crystal, keeping the springs warm and buried. In winter everything became pregnant, growing secretly, and with a strength that filled the darkness with passion. Her home glowed about her in the winter like a shell into which nothing foreign entered, nothing except the fine tense intimacies of the beings she loved, and by whom she was loved in return. She heard Olaf's voice and drew the curtains. If he came in before she had time to do it she would cry out to him: turn on the light. She came down the dark room, strung to catch the quick and lovely surprise of his face. And just as she turned on the light the door opened, and Olaf's voice was silenced and she saw, not Olaf, but Liv Evensen. It took her a second to deny her presence as a ghost: 'Liv!' she cried, 'Liv!' The girl seemed to break and bend into her arms.

'Aunt Sonja! I had to come! I had to come!'

'My child!' she said gently, all the exhilaration that she had been holding in for Olaf, forgotten, and her heart aching for the sorrow that had driven the girl, like this, into her arms. She asked no questions. Sometime Liv would tell her. 'My dear,' she said after a moment, saving her, 'it is Olaf's birthday!'

'Olaf's birthday!'

Liv said it from far away, from another country, from some realm in her spirit where no little boys had birthdays.

'Yes,' she said again, 'it is his birthday, and do look at his cake. Isn't it a beauty? The skis are copied from his own. Look close and you'll see the scratches just the same as on his!'

Liv looked close, gathering her wits from the excuse. She turned and flung her arms round the boy and kissed him, and wished him many happy days. 'I've got a bag, a bag with funny fastenings. You must have that,' she said, and looked at her aunt. 'I am sorry to have come without warning. Like this....'

Sonja broke the hesitation. She said simply: 'My dear, I did exactly the same thing,' and laid bare some fine unity between them.

Liv looked away. Beyond the lighted room, beyond the boy bent over the table, exclaiming happily and turning to his mother with outstretched arms, she saw absurd things in Paris — the way the water flushed the gutters, a saint on a street gable ... Per Malom's face in profile against the screen of acacia. His long hands had clutched the window-frame. A wonderful sunshine had flowed between and through them. It was already distant, remote in place and time to her, yet vividly present. It would last her lifetime. She would be able to evoke it out of tones in people's voices, acts, and movements, from the washing of hands, or a row of chairs, or the rumble of wheels, a line of red along a picture, the sheep on the rocks above the Sorfjorden ... anything at any time would take her ghost away and spread her senses out amongst the days that had been given to Per Malom. 'I met many people...' she began.

Sonja's hand was in Olaf's hair. She raised her eyes from the boy and gazed directly into Liv's, and saw down into the girl's desire for unburdenment: 'And one ... many, and then one! It was like that, wasn't it?'

'Yes.'

'With me there was only the one. It made it more difficult ... nobody to balance out against. Probably, Liv, the multitude was your saving.'

'I did not want to be saved....' She told the truth, confessing her full weakness. 'And it was from the multitude, the others, that I ran away.'

'You see then, they did save you!'

'I did not want to be like them.' She had taken off her fur and was stroking the fox-head. 'What is it about them, Aunt Sonja? They seem afraid to be real ... they are ruled....'

'Everybody is real.... There are, you know, Liv, different realities. It depends, perhaps, upon how much one sees. Some people see more than others.' She reflected that the girl had probably taken in a great deal, and with the full force of first perceptions unmuted by habit. It made her add, reaching instinctively towards the girl's experience, whatever it was. 'Anyhow you were wise to run away!' Liv was silent again. She turned from her to Olaf, remembering again that it was his birthday and regretting, with no lessening of sympathy for Liv, that she had been divided — taken so sharply from all that she had meant to show him and changed into the control that was demanded from her towards Liv. She could not ask Liv right out as she could, for instance, have asked Astrid: 'What is it?' Liv was not the sort who could be easily questioned. Besides, she felt no curiosity about her, only an intense understanding. She felt again in the girl that reflection of her own nature, which made her relations with her an unbearable self-judgment. The judgment was modified now by the force of her comprehension. It was not only modified for Liv but for herself. Her own experience, her 'fate' emerged from the sluggish, half-dormant pain of years into a state that resembled absolution. Looking at Liv standing so still beside the excited boy, Sonja felt that she had been a fool with herself, a hard fool. How little I know of life, after all, she admitted, with a new accepting bitterness. Beyond Liv and Olaf, across the heads of not only them, but of all her other sons and of her husband, she saw herself in Liv's place, young, and caught with love. And there was nothing to regret. She must try to make Liv see that there was never anything to regret. She said to her: 'Wouldn't you like to go up to Olaf's room and take off your things? I'll come presently.' The girl's eyes rewarded her. There came into them such a flash of release.

It seemed ages to Liv before Sonja came. She sat on the edge of Olaf's tumbled bed and buttoned and rebuttoned the linen cover of the eiderdown, grinding out her thoughts like a mill: 'I am here. I am here and he is alone. I have left him alone. I have deserted him.' He had expected her and she had not come. Now that the panic of her escape was settling, it seemed the grossest betrayal. She was a coward. She was abased before him and before her own conscience. Barbra had greater courage. She felt proud of Barbra's spirit, understanding her, as she sat on Olaf's bed teasing his eiderdown. Her humiliation was so great that it was a torture to her. She went over to the window twisting her hands. Behind the grey-blue of the trees Trangfoss fell. The water fell in a great powerful flow, no weakness in it, no wavering. The surf edged it like flowers. The summer had gone. Everything had that cold grey look to which only the snows brought redemption. She would write to Per Malom to tell him that she was here, here with the Aunt Sonja, about whom she had spoken. She would explain nothing of her flight. It was beyond explanation. If she could tell him anything it would only be that she was so unhappy, that she had had to come. She had made up her mind in a moment, hearing names she loved, in the midst of a crowd of writhing, clutching people. Fascinating — like serpents. Per Malom had had a strange look in his eyes when she had mentioned Aunt Sonja, and he had said: 'That means that there will be nothing to tell.' She remembered perfectly. It was direct of him, prophetic. It fastened her contract with him. Well! There was nothing to tell. There was only this terrible revelation within her own being that would make her different as long as she lived.

Immediately she had yielded to the impulse to return it obsessed her, blinded her to its full meaning. It was only now, when she had actually arrived, when it was clear beyond doubt that he was *there* and she was *here* that she began to take in the significance of what she had done. She had come back. Yes, she had come back. She had never, she realised now, meant to stay — not from that moment on Stortoppen when she had so valiantly declared her desire to go and had been granted such sudden permission. Some germ in her blood, some instinct as in a migratory bird had cried out to go and had been appeased by the liberty of going. She had taken the voyage, and at the end of the journey she had found Per Malom. She had found Love. He remained for her, in the midst of automata who would vanish, and he created her in his image. He was hers and she was his ... and utterly beyond possession. He would never be obliterated. In that brief spell she had reached his life — his childhood, his frustrated mother, his love for his father, his passion for the dark girl with the rose in her hair, his crazy wife and the baby that had never been born ... and all the others. The others Sasha had warned her about....

Aunt Sonja stood in the doorway. She saw the girl's locked hands, and the locked expression in her eyes as she turned and found her. She entered and shut the door. She, too, had stood like that. It took her clear to her own spell of madness and the savagery of the longing that had been unabatable. It had abated. The years, the inexorable years had gone over it. Out of it she had learned to pick up trifles. One is bent under the storm to count the grains of dust on the roadway. One learns to know trifles for trifles and see beyond them to the sum of human motives. People, she had discovered, failed one out of the aridity of their own natures, never for anything that you had done. And it was only the small mind that sat in judgment, only the little defeated souls who caught at the weaknesses of the strong as proofs of equality. There was no equality. 'Liv,' she said gently, 'tell me only what you want to tell me, but there is no need to tell me. I know. I...' she broke the dumb years that had gone over it and showed her own agony. 'I also ... we are like each other.' She felt the tremor go through Liv and pretended not to be aware. 'I felt it at once. It made me hard to you. I did not feel hard — as I must have seemed to you. The hardness was for myself, not for you.' There was silence between them like a spear, sharp with a wound fresh on it. 'I know, Liv. We are so swept down there. And when we are young, oh, my dear, it is impossible not to feel, not to ... I can't put it clearly.' She was clasping her hands very tight, keeping an outward calmness that levelled her voice and bestowed peace on the girl at her side. 'It descends upon us ... It is not of our choosing....'

'Oh, it isn't of our choosing!' the girl cried, putting out her hands and drawing them swiftly back again. 'Aunt Sonja, I feel as though my heart would break.' She turned away again towards the window.

Sonja moved closer without touching her. She did not do anything that would tear the girl's reserve. 'In that short time! It seems only like yesterday since you went away, since you were here.'

'Yes, yes.' It was only a few weeks. It was only, actually, for her, two days. Two days with Per Malom. Two days in eternity. Two days in heaven and hell. Two days in which she had run out from all shelter into the ruck of life; the battle and the hardness, racket and emergency, where men and women loved and died. They took the fine things, as Barbra took them, and enamelled them in bright hard colours to disguise them so that they would no longer be ashamed to possess them. Barbra was twisted in the hardness. She painted everything that reminded her of Norway grotesquely as a flag upon the restlessness. Cut off from it as she was now, she wondered what it was all worth — this play of life. Something was missing. But what? What a fool she was to run away from it. She said it aloud. 'I have behaved like a fool.'

Sonja was reminded that it had been her own point of view. It was a minute or two before she spoke. 'No, Liv, it isn't being a fool. It is ... taking things too deeply. I did.'

There was another pause in which their eyes met and read each other. 'I did not,' Liv said at last, slowly, 'run away, Aunt Sonja, from the depth ... it was from the others.'

'Oh!' Sonja laughed sharply, 'they are the masquerade. Don't tell me, Liv, and expect me to believe, that you were afraid of them?'

'Oh, no!'

'Well, then?'

She had nothing to say. She thought absurdly of Jacob Fuller's rams and Barbra's little red foxes. Faces out of Mina Fuller's crowd flashed before her. While she had been there, amongst them, it was herself whom she had pitied. It was she who had seemed the one to be pitied, who lacked the right quality. And now she reversed it. She spilled them all out like a cup of water and they were lost in her own fjords. Only Per Malom remained. He would remain to the end. She wondered, the wonder darted through her if he would come up here to seek her in these solitudes, to find her. What would she do then? She turned to Aunt Sonja as though asking the question, and was filled with quiet. There would be no mockery, no cheating, no pretence — for either of them — if he came. All the same, she said: 'I feel as if I had been cut in two.'

Sonja said nothing. It was true. She could not lie to herself. She had never really grown together again. Her sons had come to fill the gap in her being, to possess her with some of that measure which women need. When they would cease to possess her, if they ever did, the sense of wholeness would vanish again. She would disintegrate.... She pushed her thoughts away, and put her arm round Liv and drew her towards her.

'There is something wrong with us in this Northland, Liv. We have become like the earth we inhabit. Our natures are white as the driven snow outside and full of dark passion beneath. It is all right for us here. Here we ... we preserve our pride. When we go south, into warmer lands, we lose something of ourselves. We thaw, we flood over. We are not to blame. We have to be born down there to know how to deal with it.'

'You mean not to get broken?'

'We are too easily hurt,' she answered.

'But what are we to do?'

Sonja listened to Trangfoss, storing the music in her mind. She thought vaguely of Harald Christensen, he was only a name to her, and wondered what he could do for Liv. She let him go again. She remembered the morning of her own marriage in Trondjem. These things had nothing at all to do with Liv, for whom nothing had, in that short time, been consummated. She did not know what to say to Liv, and she said — more to herself than to the girl — with Trangfoss ringing against their ears: 'It is better, I think, to stay where we belong ... where even the trees know us....'